'What the hell do you think you're doing?'

'I treat my female guests in exactly the way their body language leads me to believe they expect,' Saul murmured, his voice as soft as velvet now. 'The invitation you posed was impossible to resist. And as for what I was doing——'

Fen's eyes went wide and wild. Her body seemed scorched by the imprint of his...

Dear Reader

What a great selection of romances we have in store for
you this month—we think you'll love them! How about
a story of love and passion, set in the glamorous world of
the movies—with deception and double-dealing to thrill
you? Or perhaps you'd prefer a romance with the added
spice of revenge...? We can offer you all this and more!
And, with exotic locations such as Egypt, Costa Rica and
the South Pacific to choose from, your only problem will
be deciding which of our exciting books to read first!

The Editor

Diana Hamilton is a true romantic and fell in love with
her husband at first sight. They still live in the fairytale
Tudor house where they raised their three children. Now
the idyll is shared with eight rescued cats and a puppy.
But, despite an often chaotic lifestyle, ever since she
learned to read and write Diana has had her nose in a
book—either reading or writing one—and plans to go on
doing just that for a very long time to come.

Recent titles by the same author:

SEPARATE ROOMS
IN NAME ONLY
THE LAST ILLUSION

WAITING GAME

BY

DIANA HAMILTON

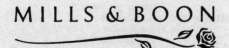

MILLS & BOON

MILLS & BOON LIMITED
ETON HOUSE, 18-24 PARADISE ROAD
RICHMOND, SURREY TW9 1SR

*MILLS & BOON and the Rose Device
are trademarks of the publisher.*

*First published in Great Britain 1994
by Mills & Boon Limited*

© Diana Hamilton 1994

*Australian copyright 1994   Philippine copyright 1994
This edition 1994*

ISBN 0 263 78689 7

*Set in Times Roman 10½ on 12 pt.
01-9410-50331 C*

Made and printed in Great Britain

CHAPTER ONE

THE group of photographers and reporters outside the highly exclusive, highly expensive West End restaurant snapped to attention as the taxi rumbled to a halt.

'You were right, they did follow.' Fenella wriggled along the seat, closer to Alex, her golden eyes smiling wickedly into his, slipping into a warm Cornish drawl as she tacked on, trying to help him loosen up, 'Brace yourself, me 'andsome!' Picking up languages had always come as easily as breathing, so regional dialects were an absolute doddle, and Alex grinned back at her.

'I'm always right, sweetheart, you should know that by now. Come on, let's strut our stuff!' He had his hand on the door release but despite his jokey tone the interior light picked out the lines of tension around his mouth.

Fenella felt her own lips tighten. At fifty-five Alex was still a handsome man, his considerable talent as a light entertainer still very much intact. She didn't know how Saul Ackerman, that hard-nosed business mogul, had the gall to try and put him down. And out.

What would he know about anything? Alex's talent was creative; Saul Ackerman wouldn't know anything about that because his head would be stuffed with columns of figures, and big profits were the name of the game.

But her triangular, cat-like smile was firmly in place again as she stepped out on to the pavement and simply stood there, illuminated by the soft lights beneath the awning, one slender hip elegantly tilted forward, her honey-gold head tipped slightly to one side, her slumbrous golden eyes almost taunting the jackals of the Press as Alex paid off the driver.

Her height gave her an advantage—helped by the ridiculously high heels she was wearing—and the tight sheath of her low-cut evening dress gave an elegant emphasis to the width of her white shoulders, the black silk clinging lovingly to understated yet exquisite curves.

As the taxi slid away the activity among the waiting Press men became frenetic as they recognised her companion. Having followed Saul Ackerman's party from the theatre, got photographs, and possibly comments from him and the leading lady he was squiring, they had probably decided to call it a day. There was only so much they could milk from a first night, a brilliant young Cornish playwright and a leading lady whose name was a household word on both sides of the Atlantic.

Her smile firmly in place, Fenella swayed over to Alex's side, felt his arm snake possessively around her narrow waist and tried not to flinch as the flashes exploded around them.

'You were at the opening, Mr Fairbourne?'

'What do you think of VisionWest's new boy genius?'

'Now Ackerman's consortium has the franchise do you see your programme continuing in the same format?'

Questions were bitten out thick and fast and Fenella gave Alex full marks for his performance. There was no sign of that tension as he picked his answer, his voice as smooth and rich as ever.

'I would hardly call Jethro Tamblyn a boy, but he is certainly a genius. As you know, VisionWest has him under contract to produce two new dramas for us a year, which will, of course, be sold to the networks. A scoop the board is justifiably proud of.'

This was common knowledge, safe stuff. VisionWest had had their own camera crew outside the theatre, making sure everyone in the west country knew that their regional commercial television station was backing the Cornishman to the hilt, Saul Ackerman, the chairman, attending the first night, wining and dining the author, his wife, and Vesta Faine, the glamorous leading lady, in high style after the performance.

'And will the networks continue to buy *Evening With Alex*? Are you worried by reported falling ratings?'

'Darling,' Fenella interjected with a tiny pout and a manufactured shiver. 'Do we have to hang round here? It's cold.'

It wasn't. The mid-May evening was unseasonably warm, if anything, but she wasn't going to see Alex savaged by this mob. She moved subtly closer to him, as if seeking his warmth, his protection. In the whole of her twenty-five years she couldn't remember needing or wanting a man's protection. But she would do anything to save Alex from having to answer that particular question.

And then a voice, coarser than the rest, heavy with salacious overtones, drawled out, 'Couldn't your wife make it tonight, Alex? Did you leave her tucked up in bed with a good book, in case she cramped your style?'

Fenella felt Alex's arm tighten around her waist and glared at the reporter who was pushing a notepad under her nose. She knew they had a job to do, a living to earn—but did they have to be so despicable?

'Jean is visiting her mother in Edinburgh,' Alex said uncomfortably. 'Now, if you don't mind——'

But they were like hounds on the scent and one of them bayed, 'And you are a keen theatre-goer, Ms——? Or is it Mrs? Or are you just a wannabe?' The voice persisted as Fenella refused to give her name. 'A model, perhaps, just itching to break into television?'

'Oh, Alex——' Fenella hid her twitching mouth against his broad, dinner-jacketed shoulder just as the flash lights exploded again.

Alex said toughly, 'That's enough. Go hassle someone else.' And he swept her forward into the luxurious foyer.

A breathing space, if only brief. While Fenella got her heartbeats back under control Alex's deep blue eyes raked her pale face with deep concern.

'You all right, sweetheart?'

'I'm fine.' Golden eyes sparkled into his. 'You did warn me what to expect. I think I could get hooked on living dangerously!'

And there was no time to say any more because they were being whisked through to the main restaurant area, all soft lighting and wickedly sumptuous décor and potted plants like a miniature exotic jungle flanking delicate Japanese silk screens painted with golden dragons with glittering ruby eyes.

And full of beautiful people. And the table they were deferentially conducted to was within spitting distance of Saul Ackerman's party. If she looked to the left of Alex's shoulder she would be staring straight into the chairman's face.

A quick, encompassing glance told her he had even more presence than she had realised when Alex had pointed him out to her during the interval back at the theatre. Somewhere in his mid-thirties, he had the type of hard, slashing features that could never be overlooked. But it was more than merely the striking combination of a strongly modelled bone-structure, thick black hair and piercing silver-grey eyes. It was the sheer unadulterated power of the man.

She didn't look his way again. She concentrated on Alex. A tiny muscle was twitching at the corner of his mouth and that only happened when he was nervous. Gently, she laid her hand over his.

'Don't worry, everything will be fine. I promise.'

'Of course it will.' There'd been only a momentary hesitation preceding his answer and then he was smiling into her eyes and he was back to being the urbane, self-confident man she loved. 'Now order something fabulous, Fen, my darling, and we'll have the best champagne on offer.'

'Well . . .' She could hear the note of doubt in her voice and deplored it. But the menu she'd been handed was almost too heavy to hold, and nothing was priced. 'Can you afford it?' Which was even more deplorable, but she couldn't help it.

'Look on it as payment for services rendered and those yet to come.' Alex leaned back expansively in his chair, the look in his eyes, the play of that smile across his mouth making her understand why women had literally thrown themselves at him during his live stage performances a decade or two ago, why his records had once regularly featured high in the charts. 'And if I can't afford it, Jean can.'

'Say no more!' Fenella buried her head in the menu. She was famished. And it was common knowledge that Jean was fabulously rich. She'd inherited a fortune from her father and was due to inherit another when her mother died. Not an event Jean was anticipating, Fenella knew, but the old lady was over ninety. So the price of a meal in a place such as this wouldn't cause Alex's wife any hardship!

'Has Ackerman noticed us yet?' Alex asked quietly as soon as he'd given their order. 'Too obvious if I turned round. I don't want him to think our being here was anything other than coincidence.' He leaned forward, trailing a finger down the side of her face. 'Look over to their table in a moment or two; make it natural. I don't think there's a man in the room who could have failed to notice you, sweetheart.'

Fenella wasn't so sure about that, but she knew the trouble Alex had gone to to discover which restaurant Ackerman intended to bring his party to tonight in time to reserve a table himself.

Strangely unwilling to meet those silver-grey eyes, she waited until the champagne was brought to their table, breaking up their intimately whispered conversation. Then slowly, as if wanting something to do while Alex's attention was no longer given exclusively to her, she allowed her eyes to wander idly over the animated group at Saul Ackerman's table.

Vesta Faine was as lovely close to as she had been on stage, her dark beauty enhanced by the dramatic lines of the white satin of her gown, her vivacious chatter obviously holding Jethro Tamblyn in thrall. The playwright was leaning forward, his arms folded on the table, his ruggedly striking features animated as he listened to every word. He looked as if he had been running both hands through his dishevelled, wiry chestnut hair for at least a couple of hours. In contrast, his wife looked out of her depth in her unimaginative chain-store dress, her pale blue eyes fixed anxiously on her famous husband. Had she married the boy from her own Cornish village when he'd been nothing more than a struggling, impecunious writer only to find him leaving her behind? Would she be able to withstand the pressures of his newly found fame?

Aware that these idle musings were merely delaying tactics, she reluctantly glanced at the head of the table. Saul Ackerman was probably just as riveted by the actress as Jethro was. But she met the silver-eyes head-

on and the mocking awareness in them made her face
go hot.

She looked away quickly, expelling the breath she
hadn't realised she'd been holding, dipping her head
on the slender stalk of her neck, feeling the long ornate
drop-earrings brush against her skin, restraining the
desire to remove the irritants. She had only worn the
outlandish things to soften the effect of her starkly
modern hairstyle. Cut very short into the shape of her
head at the back, it was long on top, falling forwards
into a honey-gold fringe that brushed her eyebrows
in a heavy, well-defined curve.

'Well?' Alex arched a brow. 'Have we been
noticed?'

Hastily banishing any trace of discomfort or
wariness from her eyes, she gave him her most brilliant smile, the discreet, muted lighting making her
shoulders gleam like oiled satin above the rich black
silk of her low-cut dress as she leaned forward, her
voice low and intimate as she told him, 'Yes. I don't
think anyone, even someone as tunnel-visioned as Saul
Ackerman, could fail to recognise your impressive
profile!'

'Never mind that.' The blatant flattery left him vis-
ibly unimpressed. 'The bastard knows every line on
my face! It's you I want him to see, Fen. I want him
to recognise you when he sees you again.' He took
her hand, rubbing his thumb across her knuckles. 'I
want him so he can't take his eyes off you.'

Involuntarily, her gaze slid to the other table and
her breath caught in her lungs. Even through the thick
veiling of her long dark lashes there was no mistaking

the speculation in those flat silver eyes. Saul Ackerman was leaning back in his chair, making no attempt now to join in the conversation that was flying around his table, the fingers of one hand idly playing with the stem of his wine glass as he watched her, his eyes unnerving.

Two thunderous heartbeats later Fenella dragged her attention back to Alex. It would appear that his wish had been granted. Ackerman would know her if he saw her again. Something fluttered inside her breasts, something uncomfortable and alien. Vowing not to look Saul Ackerman's way again, she made a determined and happily successful effort to flirt with Alex across the table but could make little impression on the superb meal she had been hungry for only a short while ago.

What a waste of Jean's money, of good food, she sniped at herself. She didn't know what was the matter with her. She would have thought it would have taken very much more than the impudent stares of a strange man to deaden her always hearty appetite.

'Won't you introduce me to your companion, Alex?'

Fenella didn't have to look up to know whom that voice belonged to. It was cool, authoritative steel, very slightly burred with dry, amused confidence. The fingers that held the fork she'd been using to push her food around her plate started to shake. Very carefully, she put the implement down as Alex hurriedly pushed back his chair and stumbled to his feet.

'Saul. How's this for a coincidence! I saw you at the theatre—only had to look for VisionWest's camera team——' His expansive smile was shaky round the edges, the sudden pinkness of his face emphasising the beginnings of a sagging jawline, the pull of gravity that was wrecking the face that had had women of all ages drooling in the aisles. He was making a too conscious effort to straighten his shoulders and pull in his stomach muscles, Fenella noted, her heart twisting with anguished love.

Ackerman, though, had no need to try to project an image. There wasn't a superfluous ounce of flesh on that tall, aggressively masculine frame. Not even the suavely styled immaculate dinner-jacket could disguise the potent rawness of this prime male animal, she thought with disgust, hating him.

He had a cruel mouth, she decided, refusing to flinch away from the eyes that were consciously and compellingly holding her own. He was totally devoid of compassion, sympathy or understanding. The un-crowned head of the consortium which had recently made a successful bid for the VisionWest franchise, he had more clout than was good for him. Already his business empire encompassed publishing, an airline, communication systems; he had forgotten the meaning of compassion—if he had ever known it in the first instance—and would break poor darling Alex without a second thought.

'How did you rate tonight's performance, Miss——?' Very briefly, his cold gaze spiked towards Alex, reminding the older man of the neglected in-troduction. No one, especially someone he had already put down as a has-been, neglected his commands.

'Fenella Flemming—my—my niece.' Alex went crimson, shifting from one foot to the other. He couldn't have looked more ill at ease if he'd tried. 'Fen, sweetheart, this is——'

'I know who it is, darling,' she cut in, sounding bored, the downward twist of her mouth, the golden glitter of her eyes letting him know she wasn't impressed, catching her breath a split-second later as she saw the gleam of pure cynicism in the blackly fringed silver eyes, the scornful knowing curve of his mouth as he repeated softly,

'Your niece? But of course—who else could she possibly be?'

Which meant, of course, that he didn't believe it for one instant.

She held his eyes with cool defiance. 'We enjoyed the performance immensely, didn't we, Alex?' She wished he would sit down, stop fidgeting from foot to foot. But maybe no one, but no one, sat when in 'the Presence'! She made a mental note to ask him some time and then went icy cold as that cool voice commanded,

'Then why don't we discuss it? Join me for coffee and brandy and I'll introduce you to the author and Vesta.'

No mention, Fenella noted sourly, of the author's wife. People wouldn't count with him unless they were famous, at the top of their own particular ladder.

'Some other time, maybe.' Fenella rose languidly to her feet, her eyes on Alex. He was probably itching to take up the invitation but not even for his sake could she endure to spend a moment longer in

Ackerman's company. One delicate brow rose and disappeared beneath her glossy, honey-gold fringe. 'It's time we were tucked up in bed, isn't it, darling?' Her mouth curved in a slow smile that couldn't be misinterpreted. 'Excuse me just for a moment while I freshen up before we leave.' And then, not giving her courage chance to desert her, she made herself encounter Saul Ackerman's icy stare. 'So nice to have met you, Mr Ackerman.'

And she walked away, heading for the rest-rooms at the rear of the restaurant, threading her way through the tables, aware as never before of the way her body swayed within the clinging confines of the black silk sheath, uncomfortably sure that the monster's eyes were following her every inch of the way.

The door closed behind her with a soft, expensive thud and she leaned gratefully against the cool, aqua wallpaper, her fingertips to her throbbing temples.

What had started out as a fun, if mentally challenging evening had ended on a quite different note, a note she couldn't really define—even if she'd wanted to. From the moment she'd learned what the chairman of VisionWest was planning to do to Alex she had disliked the man. But seeing him, meeting him, had affected her more strongly than she had bargained for.

Shuddering, she pushed herself away from the wall and effected a few minor repairs to her make-up in front of one of the softly lit mirrors. Saul Ackerman was nothing to her, simply a man she despised. He was planning to axe Alex's programme, strip him of his self-respect, toss him into an empty, financially barren future.

So it was perfectly natural that she should dislike the man so intensely. Sheer, gut-wrenching hatred was something she had never experienced before. No wonder it had a strange effect on her!

Relieved that that was sorted out, she dropped her lipstick into her slender evening purse and snapped the clasp with a defiant click. The sooner she and Alex were out of this place, back in the flat, alone together with all the time they needed to chew over the evening's happenings, the better.

She marched out into the silent, thickly carpeted corridor and almost scurried straight back in again when she saw Ackerman waiting for her, his face blank.

Sinkingly prepared to brazen it out, she gave him the ghost of an acknowledgement and stalked past him. But, levering himself away from the wall he'd been so casually leaning against, his hand shot out, clamping around her upper arm, dragging her to a teetering halt. Her breath froze in her lungs as she swayed on her impossible heels. At a distance he was lethal enough; at such close quarters he was pure poison.

'Do you make a habit of grabbing every passing female?' She managed to sound frosty but she was boiling inside, her temperature rising through the roof. How dared he waylay her? Touch her?

'Do you make a habit of being rude to strangers?' he countered, his mouth indenting sardonically. 'Or is it only me?'

'I don't know what you mean.' She glanced pointedly at the hand that manacled her arm. His fingers looked strong and lean and dark against the whiteness of her skin. 'Please let me go; you're hurting.'

'I don't think so.' There was a trace of wicked humour in his voice, making it richer, deeper, too intimate. 'I might touch the goods before I buy, but I never damage them.'

And what the hell did he mean by that? She had a sneaking suspicion but she wouldn't give him the satisfaction of asking. And there was far too much exposed flesh above the low-cut bodice of her dress to give her any hope that he had failed to register the increase of her breath-rate. And he was certainly looking, those silver eyes making a thorough scrutiny of everything exposed or otherwise.

Quickly putting a lid on her temper, she made a futile effort to pull away, hating the way the pressure of his hand increased immediately, loathing the way his touch made her feel. As if she was burning up inside. With outrage. What else?

Those wandering eyes fastened on her lips and she turned her head quickly, scanning the emptiness of the lush corridor, wishing a whole horde of other diners would come through to use the facilities.

'What do you want?' She made herself sound cool, as if nothing he had to say could possibly interest her, and heard him laugh, a warm sound low in his throat. She hadn't expected that and, just for a moment, it threw her, so when he said,

'To know who you are, for starters. There's much more you could supply me with, but that can wait,' she was unguarded enough to turn again and seek his eyes, her own wide beneath the thick golden fringe.

'You know who I am. My uncle——' her tongue tripped over the word but she ploughed quickly on before her teeth started to chatter in her head '—Alex introduced us. And if you don't mind, he'll be waiting. I——'

'But I do mind,' he cut across her. 'I didn't swallow that old chestnut. What kind of fool do you take me for? And the thought of that delectable firm white flesh tangled up with the folds and wrinkles of an ageing pop star does not bring tears of joy to my eyes.' The voice was infinitely sharper now, the silver eyes glinting like the edge of a bright steel blade.

'You're obscene!' He made her feel literally ill. 'Unc—Alex is in his prime! Pop star doesn't come into it, ageing or otherwise.'

She threw her head back, the better to glare up at him along the length of her nose, unaware that the defiant gesture afforded him an unimpeded view of her long, slender throat, the tantalisingly revealed upper curves of her breasts.

'He's a highly talented, all-round entertainer. All he needs is a new vehicle for those talents, but you're too blinkered to see it!' She drew in a great, shuddering breath, almost sobbing with the hatefulness of being held so near to that vibrant body. She had never encountered a man who exuded such power. It came off him in waves, swamping her.

But she wasn't going to drown in such a potent deluge without struggling, and she ground out between her teeth, 'VisonWest's not the only TV company in the land. There's not a damn thing stopping him from moving on and up—going where he'll be appreciated!'

'Such loyalty. I envy the man his ability to earn it,' he said grimly. The hand on her arm dropped away and his face was rigid, his eyes bitter as he subjected her to one lancing look before he turned on his heels and strode away.

Fenella knuckled her mouth, her eyes anguished as she watched the door back into the restaurant swing to behind him. Oh, God, she had probably killed off any faint hope Alex had had for his programme! She, with her big mouth, had finally wielded the axe that had been hovering over his head ever since Saul Ackerman's lot had taken over the franchise!

And even an abject, squirming apology would do no good. Ackerman's mind had already been made up. He simply hadn't got around to burying *Evening With Alex* yet. All she had done was drive the final nail in the coffin with her outspoken tongue!

She didn't know how she was going to tell Alex what she had done.

CHAPTER TWO

'I'M SORRY, you probably wanted to join Ackerman's party,' Fenella mumbled unhappily as the taxi sped towards Hampstead. Alex hadn't said a word since they'd left the restaurant and, in view of her rudeness in refusing to accept his boss's invitation, was probably deeply regretting ever having let Jean talk him into this.

'About as much as a sharp kick up the backside!' Alex sighed gloomily, giving her hand a gently reassuring pat. 'We were both brilliant, all evening, but I doubt if we could have actually sat down with them and socialised without giving the game away. We need a whole load more confidence for that.'

'I expect you're right,' she conceded, sagging back against the upholstery and closing her eyes. But she didn't feel any less miserable. Alex didn't know what had been said out in the corridor and she didn't know how she was going to tell him.

'We achieved what we set out to do—one of the sleazier tabloids will pick up on the "scandal" and splash it all over the front page. And I'll be famous—or rather, notorious—for all of five minutes. And Ackerman himself saw us together. So the old has-been who once pulled record-breaking female audiences with his sex-appeal will be judged to have regained some of his touch,' he said, sounding tired and uncharacteristically cynical. 'As they say, even bad publicity is good publicity. I thought Jean was mad when she came up with the idea but I think we were even crazier to go along with it.'

Fenella couldn't argue with that so she said nothing. But as soon as they were back in the flat her aunt Jean had bought with a minor part of her inheritance from her father she drew the curtains in the long living-room, poured her uncle a large slug of whisky and pointed him at the telephone.

'Phone her now; she'll be dying to know how everything went. I'll lay a penny to a pound she's sitting up in Edinburgh quite convinced we didn't have the bottle to go through with it because she wasn't around to make sure we did.'

Easing her feet out of her ridiculous shoes, she said goodnight and left him to it, confident that a nice long natter with his wife would cheer him up. She hated to see him so depressed. She thought the world of both of them; in some ways they meant more to her than her own parents. Which was why she'd agreed to go along with the crazy scheme in the first place— much against her better judgement.

The guest bedroom was furnished with Jean's unmistakable stamp of elegant style and home-from-home comfort. Six years ago, when her uncle had been signed up for the hour-long, prime-time *Evening With Alex*—a combination of his light-hearted interviews with celebrities from the entertainment world, plus a couple of comedy sketches and, naturally, half a dozen of his own songs performed in his own inimitable style—the couple had bought a house on the outskirts of Tavistock to be near the main studios in Plymouth.

But Alex had missed London and when Jean had received her inheritance she had immediately bought this flat, which they used when he wasn't recording his show.

They were a devoted couple, and it showed. And that, Jean had stated, was half the problem. The viewing public saw him as a middle-aged pipe, slippers and comfortable old cardigan man, never seen anywhere without his equally middle-aged and unspectacular wife. Now, if they could see him as a bit of a dog, some lovely young thing on his arm as they emerged from some rackety night-spot or other, then people might sit up and take notice, and his female audience might again tune in to his show and realise he hadn't lost all the sex-appeal that had drawn them in adoring droves in the first place!

And it might have worked, too, if she hadn't wrecked everything by the way she'd reacted to Saul Ackerman, she thought wearily, padding out of the *en-suite* bathroom packaged in an old towelling robe as she heard a light knock on her bedroom door.

'She's put us to the top of the class!' Alex was smiling now. He looked relaxed and a good ten years younger. He and Jean had never spent a night apart in the whole of the thirty years of their marriage and he was missing her.

When Jean had stated firmly that she would visit her aged mother in Edinburgh—alone—leaving the field clear for him to 'misbehave' at home he had almost vetoed the whole idea, she remembered, forcing herself to return his smile.

'Good. How is her mother?' She had only met the old lady once, years ago, and remembered her as being quite alarming, and she couldn't have changed much because Alex pulled a face as he told her,

'As intractable as ever. She still stubbornly refuses to make her home with us and insists that "Young Elspeth" can look after her. "Young Elspeth" must be knocking eighty!' He puffed out his cheeks in exasperation. 'Talk about the blind leading the blind! But never mind that; Jean's given me a whole list of things we have to do, places we have to be seen at. Shall we chew them over now, with a nice mug of drinking chocolate, or would you rather we left them to the morning?'

'They'll keep,' Fenella told him with a sick smile. Before they worked out tactics for the coming two weeks she would have to confess that they would be a complete waste of time. After her outburst to Saul Ackerman earlier this evening Alex's programme would be trashed—no matter what happened! No need to depress him tonight. Tomorrow would be soon enough.

'We did it, sweetheart!' Alex bounced into the kitchen, his arms full of newspapers. 'This one's a blinder!' He dropped a folded tabloid on the table in front of her. 'Any coffee left in that pot?'

'Plenty.' Fenella made a gulping sound in her throat. When she'd crawled out of bed half an hour ago the flat had been silent. Believing her uncle to be safely asleep, she'd sat at the kitchen table, drinking coffee and trying to decide exactly how she would tell him of her run-in with his boss.

It wasn't going to be easy, especially as he was looking so pleased with himself, delighted now because the plan to kick him back into the public eye seemed to be working.

'Well—aren't you going to read it?' He had pulled out a chair opposite her, cradling his coffee-cup, his eager grin and boyishly rumpled blond-streaked grey hair reminding her of how attractive to women audiences he had been in his heyday.

Feeling sick inside, she unfolded the paper and ran her fingers over the newsprint. Foreign wars, the balance of payments deficit and the latest cowardly IRA bomb attack had been relegated to a few square inches of print, the majority of the front page sporting the moment when the cameras had caught her hiding her mischievous smile in Alex's jacket. It came over as a snuggling embrace, Alex's arms curved protectively around her slinkily clad body and the huge caption read: "Has-Been Has-Got?"

'Don't look so shattered!' Alex grinned, swinging the paper round on the table-top, and read out the article, with plenty of hysterical expression.

Alex Fairbourne, whose top-spot TV show is to be axed—or so rumour has it—pictured outside one of London's most exclusive restaurants, finally sheds his dull-dog image. His lovely young companion coyly refused to state her name or business. Maybe his wife could throw light on the identity of the Mystery Mistress? But poor old Jean, we hear, has been conveniently banished to the wilds of Scotland. Did she go willingly, or was she pushed?

'Grief! "Mystery Mistress"! How tacky can you get?' Fenella giggled. 'But Aunty's not going to like that "poor old Jean" bit.'

'She's going to love it,' Alex contradicted. 'And since when did you ever call her Aunty?'

Since never, Fenella admitted, her face straightening out. Alex, her mother's younger brother, and Jean had always seemed more like an older brother and sister. It had nothing to do with their ages, more to do with their boundless capacity to enjoy life. Only people as perpetually optimistic as they could have devised such a scheme when faced with the persistent rumours—plus a very definite hint from Saul Ackerman himself—that *Evening With Alex* was to be axed. And, what was more, put it into practice.

And now she was going to have to tell him that she, who had promised to help, had thrown a ten-ton spanner into the works!

'We'll put in an appearance at Tinkers tonight,' Alex told her, pouring more coffee for them both. 'You won't have heard of it—how long is it since you were last in England? But it's the night-spot of the moment,' he burbled on jovially. 'The newshounds are always sniffing around, waiting for something to happen. Only a couple of weeks ago there was a deplorable fracas involving a minor Royal and a lady whose credentials are far from being unimpeachable. One of the pack earned himself quite a scoop that night. Since then there's always someone hanging around, waiting for something they can blow up into a scandal.' He pushed his chair away from the table. 'Now, what shall we have for breakfast?'

'Wait; there's something you should know,' Fenella said heavily. She felt awful. She'd let him and Jean down. She hadn't felt happy about the idea of putting on a deception for the sake of the more gutter-bound Press but once Jean had talked him round Alex had been just as enthusiastic as his wife, pointing out that Fen was the only answer—part of the family, utterly trustworthy and, almost as important, she looked the part.

'Well?' Alex prodded. 'What should I know?'

'I argued with Ackerman last night.' She took the plunge, her tongue feeling like wood. 'In the rest-room corridor, of all places. He accused me of being rude when he invited us to join his party.' She met his eyes miserably. 'And he was right. I was rude. Then I lost my head and accused him of being blinkered. I said there was nothing stopping you working with another company where your talents would be appreciated. I'm sorry if I've blown it.' She lowered her head dejectedly. 'He didn't come over as the type of man who would take any kind of rudeness or criticism lying down. There'll probably be a letter in tomorrow morning's post telling you your contract won't be renewed. So carrying on with this——' she flicked the tabloid disgustedly with her fingernail '—would be a total waste of time and effort.'

There were two more pre-recorded shows to run before the end of the current—and rumoured final—

series. He would be on tenterhooks to see if all this publicity halted the abysmally falling ratings. 'Nothing will save the show, after what I said. A flicker of public interest because you appear to be running around with a woman young enough to be your daughter won't alter a thing.'

She had said as much when her aunt had first enlisted her help but once Jean had persuaded Alex to take the idea on board there had been no dampening their enthusiastic optimism.

And no dampening now, either, she thought despairingly as Alex hooted, 'Rubbish!' and started to make the belated breakfast. All that stuff in the papers this morning had made him see himself as a celebrity again; he was, once more, the idol women had scratched each other's eyes out to be first in the queue for his autograph, a lock of his hair, the clothes off his back!

'Saul's too astute a businessman to let something like an insubordinate female affect his judgement. He was probably intrigued by the way you stood up to him. He's used to having females at his feet, not at his throat. And I'd lay odds you were the first ever to turn down an invitation from him!'

'If you say so.' Fenella was too dejected to argue. Alex might be her uncle but right at this moment she felt more like his grandmother. Pushing her fringe out of her eyes, she laid the table while he toasted wholemeal bread and scrambled the eggs; she took over as the phone in the living-room warbled out and was still half-heartedly stirring when he rushed back in again, rubbing his hands.

'What did I tell you? That was Saul on the phone—
not his secretary, mark you—the great man himself.
I am commanded to attend the open day tomorrow
in my best bib and tucker. And you, my dear Fen,
are likewise commanded! ''Bring your niece'', he
said!' He bounced over and ruffled her hair affec-
tionately then snatched the pan from the burner.
'Good God, Fen, these eggs are like case-hardened
rubber!'

But even the ruination of his breakfast couldn't
wipe the beam from his face and she felt a complete
spoiler as she pointed out, 'He doesn't believe I am
your niece.'

'Of course he doesn't. He wasn't meant to, was he?
But he still wants you along. Most insistent.'

Fen wanted to ask why but glumly decided she
wouldn't like the answer—supposing Alex knew it,
which she doubted. She asked instead, 'What is this
open day? Anything important?'

'The best news I've had in six months, sweetheart!'
Alex abandoned all attempts to eat his breakfast,
leaning back and smiling expansively. 'Part of the
studios will be open for members of the viewing public
to meet the regular presenters and the back-room
crews. It's an annual thing but this year the board,
in their wisdom, decided to throw a garden party,
issuing the invitations as if they were made of
diamond-studded gold. Much more exclusive. Backers
and advertisers in the main with a sprinkling of show-
biz names. A few selected members of the viewing
public—they've been running a competition for the
past three months. Twenty-five lucky winners re-

ceived a couple of tickets apiece. Not forgetting the performers in, and writers of, the most successful series we produce. I wasn't asked. Not until today! It's a public-relations stunt, of course—make the viewers feel part of the network. Not to mention making the invited advertisers feel important.'

'And you!' Fen pointed out with an indulgent smile. His high spirits were infectious and at least last evening's piece of rudeness hadn't produced the backlash she'd expected. That made her conscience easier.

'Ab—so—lutely!' His blue eyes were gleaming like sapphires. 'Clear up, would you, Fen? I'll phone Jean and tell her the good news. The whole thing's beginning to work like a dream. Oh, and——' he was halfway out of the room before he turned '—we'll have to scrub Tinkers tonight. Pity, but it can't be helped. We'll drive down to Tavistock this afternoon and be nice and rested for tomorrow's high jinks. Be sure to pack something sexy to wear.'

By no stretch of the imagination could the simple, wrap-over amber silk dress be called sexy, Fen consoled herself as the Daimler Jean had given Alex for his last birthday swept over the Tamar into Cornwall.

She had happily dressed for the part she'd been allotted when they'd attended the first night and shown up afterwards at the restaurant. But for some unknown reason she could no more bring herself to dress the part of a *femme fatale* this afternoon than fly. Long sleeves looked demure enough and the narrow belt was tied tightly around her waist to ensure that neither the bodice nor the cleverly draped skirt would gape.

A floppy-brimmed hat in fine amber straw, festooned with huge cream silk roses, completed the ensemble and, emerging from the guest room in the Tavistock house, she had blinked in surprise when Alex, looking very elegant and Fred Astaire-ish in a morning suit, had told her, 'You look fantastic!'

It was probably the hat, she decided edgily, not looking forward to the coming afternoon one tiny bit. Certainly nothing to do with the dress which covered her from her neck to just below her knees as effectively as a shroud.

'Don't forget to stick to me like glue,' Alex said tersely as he slowed down for the turn-off on to a decidedly minor road. 'I'm beginning to get butterflies. I'll need you to hold my hand for that reason alone.'

He was beginning to look white around the mouth, Fen noted, giving him an narrow-eyed glance as the car swept between high hedges filled with the foam of Queen Anne's lace and pink campion. It was a beautiful blue and green afternoon, as perfect as only an English early summer could be, and everything seemed to be going to plan, so why should the pair of them be so uneasy?

'I've suddenly developed a split personality,' he confided. 'One minute I'm up in the air and thinking all this is a superb idea—especially when it's bringing results—and the next I'm wishing we'd never started it. Trouble is, Fen, I can't come to terms with the thought of being on the scrap heap, reduced to earning my crust advertising somebody's frozen dinners in some ghastly commercial.'

About to point out that he didn't need to work at all, that Jean's fortune would keep them both in reasonable luxury for life, she thought better of it. Jean loved him to bits and wouldn't begrudge a penny—as the gifts she showered on him so lavishly testified. But Alex had his pride. His ability to keep himself and support his wife was important to him.

'But we won't get anywhere if we back out now. And Jean would clobber us senseless if we did,' he chuckled softly, his mood swinging again as he slowed down, looking for signposts.

Fen had imagined that the garden party would be held in some suitable spot near the main studios and the information that Saul Ackerman's country home was to be the venue had only added to the niggling sense of unease she'd been suffering ever since she'd had to admit there was no backing out, no way of rejecting the invitation to attend.

Though it was more like a royal command, she decided edgily as the high hedges gave way to a wall of rough-grained quarried stone and then to a pair of massive iron gates flung open in well-bred invitation. Uniformed men who looked suspiciously like security guards directed them along a track that branched off from the main gravelled drive to an area of grassland that served as a temporary car park.

Big white vans bearing the distinctive VisionWest logo left Fen in no doubt that the television crews would be prowling, getting the glittering occasion on film to be relayed to the viewers through the local news programme this evening. And there was well over a million pounds' worth of motorised status symbols lined up on the crushed dry grass, she noted, which meant that everyone here was a 'somebody', and that sent her tension-reading up another couple of notches.

Just why had Saul Ackerman changed his mind and invited Alex along at practically the last moment? He couldn't have had second thoughts about tossing him on to the scrap heap on the strength of a few scandal-mongering write-ups in the tabloids, surely?

Ducking her head as she got out of the car, she still managed to knock her hat to a rakish angle. Muttering under her breath, she righted it. She wasn't used to wearing any kind of headgear; she felt like a mushroom. Hitching up her skirts, she spindle-heeled her way to Alex who was pocketing the keys to the Daimler, her tawny eyes wary as she told him, 'I don't want to spoil your moment of triumph, but have you stopped to wonder why you're here? We never thought about the possibility of Ackerman being disgusted by what he must have read in the papers—he might not want to employ a man who is seen publicly to be cheating on his wife. We could be letting ourselves in for a highly public snub. Have you thought of that?'

'Yes.' Alex smoothed down his hair then took her hand and tucked it into the crook of his arm. 'It's always a possibility, but a remote one. Publicity and top ratings are the name of the game, and besides, he's no saint. He's rarely seen with the same woman twice. Whatever he is, I don't think he's a hypocrite.'

'Is he married?' Fen spiked her heels into the grass. For some unknown yet powerful reason she needed to know more about the man. A case of 'know your enemy', she supposed.

'He was.' Alex gave her a look that carried a hint of impatience. 'But it ended very messily. There was someone else involved—there always was someone else involved during the short lifetime of that marriage. Do come on, Fen!'

More cars were arriving, sunlight glittering from their faultless bodywork, more frivolous hats and sleek-faced men in morning suits. Fen gave in and fell in step beside her uncle as they gravitated towards a gateway in the fuchsia hedge, a graceful figure in the amber silk that emphasised the slenderness of her hips and long, long legs, blissfully unaware that each step she took afforded the onlooker a tiny tantalising glimpse of creamy thigh and intriguing stocking-top.

Alex's brief words had told her as much as she wanted to know about Saul Ackerman, and left her even less endeared to him than before. His poor wife was well rid of him; Alex had spoken of the marriage ending—so presumably that meant divorce. Because he couldn't keep his hands off other women? It certainly sounded like it.

Fen couldn't understand why any right-minded woman wanted to get married at all. Why put yourself in a position where your happiness depended on the good nature and fidelity of one man? Generally speaking, she liked men, enjoyed their company and valued their friendship. But she would never surrender her independence to one; she knew what it had done to her mother and, in consequence, to her. And had heard enough about disastrous marriages to make any sensible female wary.

So footloose and heart-free she would remain, a citizen of the world, a happily independent lady answerable to no one but herself.

'Fen!' A sharp nudge in her ribs brought her wandering mind back to present circumstances. Blinking, she focused on the tray of glasses, the white-shirted, impassive-faced waiter who held it. Then, champagne in hand, she took in her surroundings. Acres of emerald-green, closely mown grass quartered by stone-flagged paths, parterres of flowers cut into the sward, punctuated by tall trees, their leaves whispering softly in the gentle summer breeze. And, beyond and above the long sweep of a closely cut yew hedge a few hundred yards away, the glimpse of the tumbled roofs of an impressive Tudor house.

Some country pad, she thought sourly, contrasting it with the humble stone cottage, the only place that had ever remotely come to resemble a home, a bare twenty miles away as the crow flew.

But at least there was no sign of the owner, so be grateful for small mercies, she told herself, wondering if they could possibly manage to avoid him all afternoon.

'What do we do now?' she asked. 'Plant ourselves in front of the camera crews and grin?'

'We circulate and give each other adoring glances,' he said firmly. 'Drink your fizz; it might put you in a better mood.' He whisked her along paths and over expensively maintained lawns, mingling with various groups of guests, introducing her simply as Fenella, doing nothing at all to dampen the often openly inquisitive stares she was getting, speculative eyes watching her every move. She could almost hear them thinking, debating whether she was with Alex for love or for money.

There was a lot of well-mannered back-slapping, a lot of preening and a fair amount of talking shop and by the time they had worked their way through to the terrace beyond the hedge Fen had had more than enough.

The paving ran along the entire frontage of the spectacularly lovely house and was set with white-clothed buffet tables and bars, all perfumed and punctuated by terracotta pots brimming over with stately lilies. And in the middle distance, surrounded by a group of obvious sycophants, was Saul Ackerman.

Fen recognised him with a curious jolt right in the pit of her stomach. He was easily the most impressive male around—the handful of sexily handsome actors she had encountered notwithstanding.

Oh, drat it to Hades! She had really hoped she wouldn't have to see him. Guilty conscience, she supposed. She had behaved badly that first time they'd met. Which didn't mean she wouldn't behave twice as badly if there happened to be a second time. And that wouldn't do Alex's career prospects a whole heap of good, she admitted. But then, she had never encountered anyone, male or female, who had aroused her to such a pitch of unthinking animosity. Her blood boiled whenever she thought of him!

'We could leave now,' she whispered to Alex out of the side of her mouth. 'You must have spoken to everyone here.'

Except Saul, and she wasn't about to remind him of that. She was sick of being on show, being talked about. Most of the people here would have read at least one scandal-mongering piece of so-called journalism. Most of the men, with varying degrees of interested speculation, had ogled her, while she was sure all the women were bitching about her inside their heads. She was getting paranoid, she recognised, but that didn't stop her wanting to hit Alex when he scoffed, 'What, and miss out on all that gorgeous food? Besides, I haven't paid my respects to Saul yet. Got to keep a high profile. If Jean were here she'd say the same.'

'Go ahead,' Fen told him, feeling tight-lipped. 'You'll deserve a medal if you can drag him out from under all those female admirers.' She had just recognised the lushly sensual, scarlet garbed figure of Vesta Faine hanging adoringly on to his arm. No doubt she was his current lady. Seen twice already in his company, she must be all set to break the record—if what Alex had said about the staying power of his ladies was true. 'And I need to go to the loo,' she grumbled untruthfully. 'Where is it?'

'Go to the house. You'll find doors if you look for them. Saul won't have Portakabins labelled "His" and "Hers" on his sacrosant property.' He gave her arm a little squeeze. 'Don't be long. I'll get us some food and try to grab Saul's attention. After all, he did expressly invite you to come.'

Which wasn't what she wanted to hear, Fen thought as she swayed her way along the terrace, skirting the lily pots and knots of festively dressed personalities with an empty smile fixed on her face.

She had no need to find a bathroom—just a bit of empty space. And she had no intention of returning before she had got herself nice and calm again. Alex could manage on his own; she'd done quite enough.

To the side of the house she found a swimming-pool complete with loungers and white-painted wrought-iron tables. And people. Quickly, she withdrew her inquisitive nose from the trellis of billowing roses that formed part of the pool surround and explored further.

And eventually found just what she'd been hoping for: utter seclusion. A small secret garden, enclosed on three sides by tall yew hedges, the fourth side open to a vista of sweeping fields and the thickly wooded river valley below. No one in sight. Just the sun, the warm soft air, the patchwork of greens, the song of the birds. Heaven.

Ignoring the stone bench seat, strategically placed for peaceful contemplation of the breathtaking view, she kicked off her shoes and sank down on the soft, sun-warmed grass, pulling her hat down over her face to shade her creamy pale skin from the damaging rays.

If she weren't so tense she would be asleep within seconds; she hadn't realised just how exhausted she was. The past four years she'd been travelling round Europe, flitting from one job to the next like a demented gnat, enjoying every hectic moment. Eighteen months ago, after her father's sudden and unexpected death from a heart condition, she had taken two months off to get her distraught mother settled with an old schoolfriend—recently widowed herself—in Australia. And that had been no easy ride.

She had grieved for her father, of course she had, her sorrow taking the form of deep regrets. Regret that he had barely ever acknowledged her existence and, when he had, only because of her nuisance value. A selfish man, there had been no room in his life for anything outside his work as a highly respected travel writer. He'd travelled the world, dragging his wife along behind him and, much later, the child he had never expected or wanted. Not that he'd had to drag his wife, exactly. She'd been too dependent on him, too besotted, to let him out of her sight! And now that he had gone, her mother didn't know what to do with her life. So no, that two months spent trying to help her mother come to terms with the loss she vowed she would never be able to accept had not been a picnic.

And a few weeks ago, during one of the frequent calls to Australia she made from wherever she happened to be, her mother had instructed mournfully, 'When you're next in the UK I want you to arrange for the cottage to be sold. I couldn't bear to go there again, not without your father. It would kill me. You can crate up any of his books and papers that are still there and send them out to me. I'd ask Alex and Jean, but you know how busy they are. Alex has better things to do with his time than bother himself with my affairs.'

And so, after a job that had taken her to the English Midlands, Fen had dropped in on Jean and Alex in Hampstead, intending to spend a few days with them before hiring a car and driving down to Cornwall, promising herself that before she did anything about disposing of the cottage and its furnishings she would give herself a full week simply to laze around and recoup her energies. Instead, she had found herself drawn into playing the part of Alex's mistress, all thoughts of a much needed breathing space pushed into the background.

Sighing gustily, she wriggled herself into a more comfortable position, feeling her skirt ruck up around her thighs and not caring. There was no one to see her, after all. If she was going to have to spend the next couple of weeks racketing around notorious night-spots with her uncle, pretending they were having an adulterous fling, she would need to unwind.

She made a conscious effort to relax, to push everything out of her mind, and succeeded, feeling her body go boneless, sleep pulling at her eyes, pulling her deeper and deeper . . .

'Can anybody join in, or is Alex the only man who's allowed to sleep with you?'

The steel-sharp voice cut through the layers of sleep as a hand flicked the silk and straw confection away from her face. Fen went rigid with shock, then wriggled frantically, trying to get upright without sacrificing too much of her dignity. But a warm hand— a burningly warm hand—on her thigh sent all thoughts of dignity scattering in the ether, her temper and temperature going through the roof.

Not only had her skirt rucked up to an indecent level, it had also gaped embarrassingly. And that lean, olive-toned hand was curved around her thigh, on the soft white flesh above her stocking-top.

'How dare you?' She slapped fiercely at his hand, but it didn't budge an inch. The pressure of his fingers increased by a fraction and Fen pulled in a scorching breath, appalled by the electrifying sensations that spread all over her body. Then she twisted away, ending up on her hands and knees, hardly knowing how to contain her fury when he simply reached for her, dragging her down on to the grass, his arms pinioning her beneath him.

Down, but not out, she glared into his unsmiling eyes and tried to control her hectic breathing as she rasped out, 'What the hell do you think you're doing, Mr Ackerman? If this is a sample of the way you treat your female guests I'm surprised you weren't locked safely away years ago!'

And then he did smile, a sweet, slow smile that took her breath away all over again, a smile that touched his eyes like the rays of the moon on a silver sea and made the harshly modelled planes of his face seem far less uncompromising.

'I treat my female guests in exactly the way their body language leads me to believe they expect,' he murmured, his voice as soft as velvet now. 'The invitation you posed was impossible to resist. And as for what I was doing——' He moved off her and her eyes went wide and wild. Why, her body seemed scorched by the imprint of his, as if she would never be able to rid herself of the way all that power-packed virility had felt as it had crushed her into the grass! 'I was looking for you. Alex has been going frantic. And having found you, pinned you down so to speak, I wasn't willing to risk losing you again.'

He got to his feet, as if nothing had happened, as if he tumbled women he barely knew in the grass every day of the week, insulted them and put his hands... Oh, it was unendurable! And if he touched her again she would kill him!

But she didn't. Because when he hauled her to her feet, and smoothed down her wrinkled skirt, pulled together the gaping bodice of her dress and settled her silly hat on her head, his touch was completely impersonal, as if he were dressing a tailor's dummy, making it fit for the public gaze. And that, strangely, was miff-making enough without his almost curt command, 'Come. Alex has something he wants to tell you. Besides, if you're missing for much longer he'll get withdrawal symptoms.'

CHAPTER THREE

SAUL didn't touch her as he walked her back to the party, not even a hand beneath her elbow as they mounted the flight of stone steps that led up from the lower walkway to the pool and terrace level.

Which didn't mean a thing. Because Fen couldn't have been more aware of him if his hands had been all over her. Her body was burning, her mouth suddenly dry, her breath thick in her lungs. Yet she was shivering, quivering all over like a startled mare. But that was just a symptom of the tension she'd been under ever since she and Alex had started out on this mad charade, she informed herself tartly, trying to wipe away the memory of being pinned beneath Saul Ackerman's hard male body, the way his hand had felt on the soft warm flesh of her thigh.

But the memory wouldn't go away and she had never been as pleased to see anyone in her life as she was to see Alex when he met them at the end of the now almost deserted terrace.

'So there you are!' His face lit up with relief. 'I thought you'd run out on me, sweetheart.'

'Never!' In her eagerness to reach him and the safe normality he represented, one of her spindly heels twisted beneath her and only Saul's lightning-fast reactions, the hand that snaked out to steady her, prevented her from falling in a heap and saying goodbye to what little was left of her dwindling composure. 'If you're this eager in bed I can understand why he hates you to be out of his sight,' Saul murmured close to her ear, his breath fanning her thick honey-gold fringe beneath the dipping, rose-laden brim of her hat.

Fen shuddered with scalding outrage. She wanted to tell him to shut his insulting mouth but the words wouldn't come. Her tongue was stuck to the roof of her mouth. And the hand that had steadied her relaxed, just a little, his thumb making lazy circles on the inside of her arm, scorching her through the thin silk sleeve. And the most bewildering, the most horrible thing of all was the way she was just standing there as if turned to stone, letting him do it. Enjoying——

No! Never!

She slapped that thought away smartly then went hot all over as he released her arm, his hand brushing her silk-clad bottom as it fell back to his side, brushing against her so lightly that she could almost have imagined it.

'Excuse me for a moment; there's someone I must have a brief word with,' Saul said, turning away, his movements very fluid for a man whose body packed so much power. And Fen gave him a sourly reluctant ten out of ten for urbanity, for behaving as if nothing had happened, as if he hadn't foully insulted her with both word and touch!

'Can we go now?' Fen glared at her uncle, unfazed by the way his eyebrows shot up to his hairline at her tone. He hadn't been close enough to catch Saul's low-voiced insult, and the touching had gone on out of sight!

'Not yet.' Alex pulled her out of the way of the waiters who were already dismantling the buffet tables. The party was long over. She must have slept for longer than she'd thought. 'Listen,' he began in a rush, his flushed face close to hers, 'while you were missing I had a word with Laurence Meek—he's the director of programmes, the man who can put 'em on and take 'em off. And the only living soul who can sway the decisions he makes is——'

'Saul Ackerman,' Fen put in drily, hatred bubbling up inside her all over again at the mere thought of him.

'Dead right. Anyway, Laurence gave me a very strong hint that, after all, my show mightn't get the shove. His actual words were, "Don't go anywhere else with your c.v., old man. There's a big decision in the offing and I think it will go your way."'

'That's great news!' Fen's golden eyes shone, her bad mood disappearing like mist in the summer sunshine. She was really pleased for him. His own show meant a lot to him—his pride, his self-respect, his sense of worth. Slowly, she walked over to the stone balustrading that edged the terrace and gazed out over the now deserted gardens, Alex at her side. His good news meant that soon they would be able to stop the pretence of a torrid, adulterous relationship. She had never been wildly ecstatic about the idea but she hadn't foreseen how tawdry and besmirched it would make her feel. The relief was heady.

The Ackerman monster certainly had a beautiful home, she decided, the tranquillity of the scene soothing her. She could almost imagine herself putting down roots if she owned something like this. Almost. She sighed. No, she couldn't see herself putting roots down anywhere, any time. She couldn't really see the point. There was always something new over the horizon, something to draw her wandering feet onwards . . .

'And when's this big decision to be taken?' she asked.

'I'm not sure. But soon. And when it's made, either way, we can drop this act.'

'But it can't have had anything to do with their change of mind, surely?' Fen looked at him worriedly. 'One scandalous story in print . . .' Her voice trailed away. From what she'd gathered, the viewing figures for Alex's show had been falling steadily for some time, and dropping like a stone just recently. Could their altered decision be based on what was, after all, simply a piece of sleazy journalism and salacious speculation? It didn't make a whole lot of sense.

But Alex didn't care why he had been offered a reprieve, only that it seemed that he had. He was smiling expansively, his face too flushed. Fen suspected he'd been celebrating ever since he'd had that talk with the director of programmes. The champagne had been flowing like water, after all!

'Shall I drive us home?' She didn't want to offend his male pride by suggesting he might be over the legal limit—well over!—but it was time they made a move.

She didn't want to face Saul again, not after what he had said and done. Especially not after what he had said and done!

'We'll see. Later. Saul's asked us to stay to dinner—I've been trying to tell you.'

'What?' Fen shook her head decisively. 'No. Oh, no!' She had had more than enough of his company. Several others would have been invited, too, she was sure of that. A select few. Definitely including the lovely Vesta Faine! But she had no wish whatsoever to be part of the élite around Saul Ackerman's dinner-table tonight.

'Fen!' Alex looked pole-axed. 'Don't be like that! I know it's been difficult—being taken for my mistress, and everything. But it won't be for much longer, I promise, and then we can come clean. And it's important to me; you must see that. We got away with refusing his invitation once; do it twice and I can kiss all hopes of a change of mind goodbye!' He put his hand over hers as it clenched and curled around the sun-warmed stone. 'I can't afford to ruffle his feathers, at least not until that decision's been made. And he might want to discuss it over dinner. Please, sweetheart, try to endure it. For me?'

It was emotional blackmail and she knew she had no choice. But, just to get her own back, she snapped out, 'Couldn't we just tell him we can't wait to get back to your place and dive into bed?' Saul would understand something like that—the arrogant, insulting, over-sexed monster...!

She saw Alex's face go purple, and knew why when, from just behind her, that hated voice said, in a tone like steel cutting through stone, 'Shall we go in? We've time for a drink before dinner. And perhaps your niece . . .' his voice hovered damningly over that word ' . . . would like to freshen up before we eat?'

He had heard what she had said; no doubt about it. Trying to hide her flaming face beneath the brim of her hat, she had no other option but to keep pace with the two men as they walked towards the house. But once inside she could have wept with relief as he introduced his housekeeper, Mrs Pringle.

'Show Fenella to the blue guest room, Prinny. And hold dinner for an hour, would you? We'll be watching VisionWest News in the den.'

How many others would be watching, too? How many invited guests for dinner? Would they all be wondering what she and Alex got up to in bed? Wondering if his wife knew exactly what was going on?

Fen felt dreadful. She wasn't cut out to be a mistress, even a pretend one! Hysterically, she wondered if she could tell the housekeeper she'd got a sick headache and was going to have a nice lie-down. No, she would never get away with it. Saul Ackerman would be up like a shot to soothe her fevered brow. He probably knew a few good variations on the game of doctors and nurses!

Oh, she was getting sex on the brain! she howled at herself after the housekeeper trotted off, having deposited her, as ordered, in the blue room. She, who rarely gave the subject a moment's thought in her busy, restless life, preferring to be celibate rather than risk catching some dreadful disease. In any case, she didn't know what the fuss was about. She'd tried it once and had found it to be about as exciting as reading the back of a bus ticket.

True, she'd been only eighteen at the time. Eighteen and lonely, during her first year working for her degree in modern languages. The other female students had all fancied Ray Gordon, but he had picked her and it had gone to her head. She had imagined herself in love with him, and he banished the loneliness, and she had fancied herself as a modern, liberated woman, with a partner—modern women didn't use words like 'lover' and 'mistress'. But six weeks after their first date he had taken her back to his flat and into his bed. And she'd hated every moment of it and had decided that, after all, she didn't need a partner, not if it entailed putting up with all that rather embarrassing business between the sheets.

She would rather handle her life all by herself, make it how she wanted it. With her first-hand knowledge of other countries, their customs and languages, she could be as fancy-free as she chose, and she need never be lonely while there were places to go, people to meet, while she kept a lively, enquiring mind in her head.

So why did sex keep raising its contentious head now? Nothing to do with Saul Ackerman, the way he had touched her? No, of course not. She despised and hated the man.

Tossing her hat on the graceful half-tester bed, she scanned the room sourly. Blue. A misty, pale blue combined with soft greys and cream. Very tasteful. Rather fine antiques, too. But, what was more to the point, an elegantly appointed bathroom with everything a female guest might need to help her freshen up for the fray. For fray it would be, she acknowledged as, twenty refreshing minutes later, she reluctantly made her way back downstairs.

Not knowing where to go, she stood for a few moments in the centre of the huge, jonquil-scented hall. There were big bowls of the delicate, late spring flowers everywhere. And there was an undertone of beeswax, too, and carefully tended great age. The mellow panelling seemed to surround her protectively and the lovingly polished antique furniture looked like old and valued friends. It was a house that had lived through history, sheltering many souls through the ages, and it seemed to welcome her, offer her a gracious, gentle haven . . .

'Through here, miss.'

Fen blinked rapidly. It wasn't like her to come all over fanciful. In fact, it was unheard of. She was probably the most level-headed person she knew.

'Thanks.' She summoned a wavery smile for the housekeeper who had just come through one of the doors, a tray of used glasses in her capable hands. 'I was a bit lost.'

Lost in a load of nonsense, she informed herself witheringly. A house was a house, when all was said and done. Nothing to get all dewy-eyed about! Trying not to look as apprehensive as she felt, she approached the door Mrs Pringle was patiently holding open for her. From the number of the glasses on that tray there must be quite a crowd through there.

Bracing herself to endure more speculative looks and loaded questions, Fen took a deep breath and sailed into the room, her eyes going wide as she saw Alex sprawled comfortably in a leather club chair, a glass in his hand, Saul on a two-seater sofa, and not another soul.

Alex was too intent on the TV set to have noticed her but Saul got immediately to his feet, motioning her to the sofa as he moved to the drinks tray.

Fen's eyes raked the room for somewhere else to sit and decided that perching herself on the edge of the hard-backed oak chair by the bookshelves, removing the stack of what looked like high-quality trade magazines in order to do so, would look childishly defensive.

She had nothing to be defensive about, she assured herself, sinking down on to the sofa. So she wasn't going to act as if she had. It was a comfortable, booky room, very relaxing, and the fact that she didn't have to face a horde of other guests was an enormous relief. She took the flute of champagne Saul handed her with a cool murmur of thanks and watched him top Alex's whisky glass to the brim and wondered just what it was about the man that made her come out in goose-bumps whenever she looked at him.

He had discarded the jacket of the formal suit he'd been wearing this afternoon, removed his tie, and the crisp white fabric of his shirt skimmed wide, hard-boned shoulders and the dark, close-fitting trousers emphasised his tall leanness. He was a sexy-looking brute, she admitted, taking a gulp of champagne to moisten her dry throat. He had the look of a man who would never take no for an answer, had probably never had to even try. He blatantly exuded that type of arrogance.

Perhaps that was what made him appear so dangerous—that and the way he moved, the way his eyes seemed to be able to reach right inside her head and read her thoughts, the way the hard mouth could suddenly, unexpectedly smile and make the recipient believe the sun had come out, shining brilliantly just for them, on even the darkest, dreariest of days.

But the threat he posed was not to herself; how could it be? As far as she was concerned he was no threat at all! No, it was Alex she had to think about. The threat to his programme, his standing in the entertainment world. So she would try to forget the brute's insults and do her best to be cool and polite, and eat his wretched dinner and say goodnight and goodbye very nicely, like a well-brought-up young lady. For her uncle's sake.

She shot the object of her concern a frowning look. And he caught it as he momentarily looked away from the screen, lifting his glass in an absurd salute and grinning foolishly. He was drinking far too much. She would definitely have to drive him home. She wished Jean were here to take him in hand. His hoped-for reprieve had gone to his head and knocked out all his common sense!

As Saul joined her on the sofa Fen braced herself. If he tried to touch her again she would scream! But he simply topped up her champagne and concentrated on the small screen.

Fen sipped and tried to convince herself that the crackle of electricity between them existed only in her

imagination, that her minute awareness of him was a
perfectly natural reaction to the insults he had heaped
on her. She had every right to be wary of him after
the things he had said and done. But once dinner was
over they could leave and she would never have to see
him again.

On that comforting thought, she, too, concentrated
on the screen. After the commercial break the second
half of the regional news programme began and she
watched without much interest the shots of members
of the viewing public being shown around some of
the studios. And only when the scene shifted to the
garden party did she begin to sit up and take notice.

As an exercise in corporate back-slapping it was very
well done. Loads of famous faces looking as if they
were having a whale of a time and the director of programmes explaining just how many exciting packages
the viewing audiences could look forward to in the
future. But in the background of many of the shots
she could see herself and Alex, she clinging to his arm
as if glued to his side and—horror of horrors!—every
step she took revealed an outrageous glimpse of legs
and stocking-tops.

And she had congratulated herself on managing to
dress so demurely! Her face on fire, she surrep-
titiously tugged at the traitorous wrap-over skirt and
hoped she had imagined the wicked, low chuckle at
her side.

'Marvellous publicity!' Alex slurred as the credits
began to roll. 'Great idea of yours, ol' man!'

And not bad publicity for him, either, Fen thought
sourly. There wouldn't be many viewers who would

have missed the sight of Alex Fairbourne with a doting dolly on his arm, flashing her legs and smiling dotingly into his handsome, distinguished face.

'The idea was a collective one,' Saul said dismissively. But there was not a hint of the expected censure in his tone. He sounded faintly amused, indulgent even. Fen wondered what he was up to because he didn't seem the type to suffer tipsy maunderings from an underling gladly.

'Shall we go through?' Saul rose to his feet, pressing a bell-push discreetly hidden away at the side of the stone fireplace. 'Prinny will be serving dinner.'

She would be now, Fen thought tartly. The housekeeper had probably been waiting, like an athlete on the starting-block, for just such a summons. Putting her glass down on a side-table, she noted with mild shock that it was empty again. How many glasses of champagne had she gulped her way through? How many times had he silently topped the thing up?

And Alex was definitely unsteady on his feet as Saul ushered them into a small, intimate dining-room that had open French windows leading out on to the terrace. And throughout the beautifully served and prepared meal Saul kept the wine flowing.

One glass was all Fen allowed herself and Saul, she noted, had scarcely touched his. Was he deliberately trying to get his guests drunk? she wondered hysterically. But what would be the point?

Whatever his host's intentions, Alex was definitely under the weather. Twice she had kicked him under the table but it hadn't made a scrap of difference to his alcoholic intake. She would have to pour him into the car! That was if she could ever get him to stop talking!

And it was all Saul's fault! He was the one who was plying the wine, leading poor old Alex on to talk about past triumphs, the celebrities he'd met in his long and—up until fairly recently—successful career. He was being manipulated, made to feel fêted and important. Fen would have dearly liked to shove one of those dratted wine bottles right down Saul Ackerman's throat!

She didn't know what he was up to, only that it was something despicably devious, and she was proved horribly right when, coming through with the coffee, Prinny was instructed in that 'won't take no for an answer' voice, 'Show Mr Fairbourne to his room, would you? He's had a long day.' He got to his feet with a movement that combined ease with purpose and helped his almost paralytic guest to stand upright. 'That's all right with you, Alex? I wouldn't want one of our star performers to fail a breath test.'

'His' room! Thus implying that the housekeeper had known the guests would be overnighters. Oh, the tricky bastard! And Alex said nothing, not a word, just gave her a cross-eyed, fatuous smile before staggering out behind the stone-faced Mrs Pringle. He would fall asleep repeating that 'one of our star performers' like a litany, she just knew he would, the poor old love. Saul Ackerman had been using him, playing on his insecurities. And she thought she was beginning to understand why!

So when Saul turned back to her after closing the door behind his inebriated guest and his housekeeper she was already on her feet.

'Thank you for dinner, Mr Ackerman.' Never let him be able to accuse her of having no manners again! 'I'll collect Alex in the morning. About eleven?'

Her uncle wouldn't have surfaced much before then, the state he was in. And by then Ackerman should be about his business, stamping around, playing God around one of his business enterprises. The haughty glare she gave him belied the way her heart was thumping about. His reaction would tell her whether her suspicions were true, and the tiny, frozen moment of utter silence was straining her composure to the limit.

And then that breathtaking smile, those molten silver, magnetic eyes. Fen shuddered, pulling in air, and Saul said softly, 'How unnecessary, Fenella. You'll be staying, too. Or hadn't I mentioned it?' He moved closer, his nearness intimidating. She stood her ground, her pride not allowing her to give way. He knew damn well he had mentioned no such thing. 'I wouldn't like to see you up on a drink-drive charge, either.'

One insult too many! Fen's nostrils flared. He really was despicable!

'I'm within the legal limit,' she snapped at him, not so sure about that, though. She'd had one glass of wine with dinner but couldn't be positive about the amount of champagne she'd gulped down while they'd been watching that programme. And she felt perfectly clear-headed. In any case, if she had any doubts at all, she was perfectly prepared to drive to the nearest lay-by and sleep in the car.

'Debatable.' His purring voice underlined her own doubts and her eyes fell from his. Immediately, she felt more sure of herself. He couldn't make her stay. But, 'Sadly—or not—it depends on the way you look at it——' the fingers of one hand brushed her thick fringe away from her eyes '—Prinny has a streak of Puritanism a mile wide, so, for the sake of the proprieties, you and Alex have separate rooms. Not——' his fingers slid down the side of her face, feathering along her jawline '—not that he would be much good to you tonight.'

Fen choked. She felt as if she was drowning in agitation. All down to the way he was touching her, his insults. Not that he would think of them as insults, of course. Everyone was supposed to believe that she was having an affair with Alex. But that didn't excuse him!

She jerked her head away but he moved closer, much closer, and she found herself backed against the table with nowhere else to go. About to tell him she had no intention of staying under the same roof as him, she opened her mouth to yell at him and found the words pushed back into her throat as he laid a silencing finger against her lips.

And she didn't know whether her stunned and shattered inability to move a muscle was due to the way her senses were swimming at the intimacy of his touch, or the way he imparted conversationally, 'Let me warn you against refusing my hospitality again, Fenella. You wouldn't want me to feel insulted, would you? It might make me take my understandable feelings of pique out on your ''uncle''. And that would be a shame, especially after I've convinced Laurence Meek that we should reconsider our decision to cut such dead wood as *Evening With Alex* out of our schedulings. Shall we take our coffee out on to the terrace?'

CHAPTER FOUR

ALMOST spitting with outrage, Fen flounced down on to one of the sumptuously upholstered patio chairs and watched Saul put the tray of coffee things on the white-painted wrought-iron table. While he poured, she brooded.

Out-and-out blackmail. Do as I say, or else . . .

Do as I say. And no Brownie points for guessing what that might be! He probably thought she was a career-mistress; had seen her with Alex, fancied her, and decided he wanted a piece of the action for himself!

She remembered precisely how many times he had touched her, and where, and how. Her skin tingled, all over her body, and she was sure her face had gone scarlet. And if he so much as laid one finger on her she would scream the house down. Hadn't he imparted that Mrs Pringle had a mile-wide Puritanical streak? She would come to her rescue, surely she would? In any case, she would scream her lungs out until she did!

But he didn't attempt to touch her, or make any further insulting remarks about bed. He put her coffee in front of her, offered cream and sugar, which she stiffly declined, and sat down opposite, leaning back and looking enviably relaxed.

'So—tell me something about yourself.' No trace of steel in his voice now. It was liquid gold as it trickled into her consciousness, making her nerve-ends tingle all over again. And he sounded as if he was truly interested, and that, she assured herself, was simply a trick of the seasoned womaniser's trade.

But, what was worse, she almost wanted to talk to him, relax with him in the soft, flower-scented evening. But only almost. She wasn't that much of a fool. And, in any case, the desire, if indeed it was there, had come fleetingly into being merely because she was sick and tired of the deception, the part she was playing.

'Why?' The question was baldly put and cold, letting him know she wouldn't be that easy to trick. She braced herself for an abrasive return to her far from subtle put-down and found herself gaping at him, flummoxed, as he told her softly,

'Because I'm interested; why else would I want to know anything at all?' In the mellow light spilling from the open French windows behind them she could see the amused slant of his mouth. He shifted into a more comfortable, fluid position, his long legs stretched out in front of him, the diluted light out here on the terrace painting the austerity out of his memorably attractive features. He looked completely, utterly lazy, contentedly at peace with himself. In complete contrast to the slashing authoritarian she'd come to expect. 'Or maybe intrigued is the more apposite word,' he suggested, his eyes drifting in her direction, silvery and soft and beguiling. 'Whatever.' A minimal shrug that barely moved the soft white fabric that covered his hard, wide shoulders. 'I want to know all there is to know about you.'

He was, she recognised hollowly, beginning to fascinate her. And that didn't feel comfortable.

'Then want must be your master.' How many times had she heard her mother say that? Every time she had childishly tried to wiggle her way past the blinkers that had effectively cut out everything, even her own daughter, enabling her to concentrate her entire attention on her slavishly adored husband.

Fen smiled fatalistically at the memory, and that softened the rebuff, made her voice marginally less tart as she added, 'There's really very little to tell.'

'That can't be true.' He lifted his arms and crossed them behind his head, the watchful silver eyes never leaving her face. 'Let's kick off with where you live, shall we? You must have a bolt-hole you go to when you're between lovers.'

Anger shook her like a rough hand and the only thing that kept her in her seat was the memory of the reluctant promise she'd made to Jean. She'd agreed to help Alex by going along with this hateful charade and she wished to Hades she had flatly refused.

'Nowhere special,' she mumbled, finishing the last of her coffee and placing the wide-bowled cup back on its saucer with a hand which shook with all that pent-up inner ire. And that was the truth because she went where her work took her, never stayed anywhere long enough to make anything remotely resembling a settled home.

'Then let me put it another way.' Suddenly, he looked taut and dangerous, and the thread of steel was back in that honeyed soft voice. 'What will you do and where will you go when Alex tosses you out? We can dispense with the polite fabrication of a blood tie, don't you think?' There was no hint of laziness in his pose now. He hadn't moved a muscle but he still looked like a tiger ready to pounce and snarl and rend her apart. 'And he will ask you to leave, you know. You are simply an aberration. Put it down to the male menopause, if you like. One thing is for sure, though. Deep down he's devoted to Jean. He would never leave her. But then, I'm sure you already know that. Women who—attach themselves to much older, married men—preferably men in the public eye with money to throw around—usually know the score.'

Not even for the sake of Alex's career would she put up with this! She stumbled to her feet.

'You assume far too much! I take it I'm to use the blue guest room,' she said harshly. 'Goodnight, Mr Ackerman. I wish I could say I'd enjoyed the evening. But I haven't.'

He was on his feet just as suddenly, moving in on her, blocking her way. This close, he was far more than merely disturbing and when he touched her, his hands closing round her elbows, she knew she couldn't have moved even if she'd wanted to. Her head was spinning, her legs shaky and she raised wide, disconcerted eyes to his as he reminded her silkily, 'You haven't answered my question. What will you do? Where will you go when Alex comes to his senses?'

It had been on the tip of her tongue to ask what made him think Alex was her lover. Silly question! She knew exactly why he and the readership of a few trashy tabloids thought that! She was going to have to watch her tongue around him. The trouble was, his hatefulness drove everything sensible out of her head. Glaring at him, she amended glacially, 'What makes you think I have lovers in the plural? Maybe Alex is the one and only. Have you thought of that? And take your hands off me.'

He ignored her request, his eyes gleaming in his shadowed face as the pressure of his fingers increased just a little.

'How old are you? Twenty-four? Twenty-five? Don't tell me you reached that age in a state of blissful chastity, Fen, because I won't believe it. Not with your looks, that aura of sexual excitement you carry around with you. Plenty of men must have made a play for you.' His voice was suddenly huskily seductive and she shivered uncontrollably, unconsciously lapping her dry lips with the tip of her tongue, a revealing gesture he didn't miss. 'Don't tell me our ageing pop star was the first man you allowed past first base.'

He was crude. He was a devil. And she hated him!

'It's none of your damned business, is it?' Her tone was passionately acid. 'You deliberately made Alex drunk, forced us to stay here——' She broke off jaggedly, her words choking her, and he gave a soft laugh and pulled her slowly against the hard length of his body, his arms sliding around her as he said with a fierce tenderness that utterly bemused her,

'He made himself drunk. He's been under a lot of strain recently. The guy was celebrating. Why should I try to stop him? Poor baby...' One of his hands slid up to cradle the back of her head, easing it forward to rest against the hollow of his shoulder. 'If you thought I'd plotted to make him incapable, just to get you alone and jump on you, forget it. I don't operate that way.'

Didn't he? Had she misjudged him? No, how could she have done? She hadn't forgotten the insults he'd handed out, even if he had. And what was she doing here, staying so passively in his arms, breathing in the subtle male muskiness of him?

Alarm bells jangled in her brain and her mouth went dry as, agitatedly, she wrenched her head back, dragging herself away as she asked crossly, 'Just how *do* you operate?'

'Ah.' His eyes gleamed wickedly. 'Have patience. You'll find out.' Slow words, softly spoken, slow, soft movements of his hands as they slid down to prevent her wriggling attempts to distance herself, pressing against the small of her back, anchoring her lower body to the masculine jut of his pelvis.

Fen's eyes went wide with shock, her body going totally still. The heat of all the world seemed concentrated in that one region, explicitly concentrated. She simply couldn't believe such a sensation possible, couldn't believe the scorching heat that seared through her loins and made her ache with something she had never experienced before, forcing her to recognise instinctively that the only way to assuage that ache was to press her body closer to his, closer . . .

'Let's say, for now, that friend Alex is walking a very thin line indeed and you would do well to remember it. Shall we have more coffee and resume our conversation?'

She heard his words as if from a great distance and when he released her she felt disorientated, her veins still running with fire and anguish. It was as much as she could do to stay upright and, more out of necessity than desire, she sank back down on to the chair and inwardly cursed him for being such a bastard.

He was as good as telling her that he called all the shots and, until a decision had been reached on Alex's future with VisionWest, she supposed he did. And yes, she would do well to remember it. She and Alex had come this far with their distasteful charade, and she, personally, had endured much that she would have preferred not to. It would be an appalling waste of effort if she were to tip the balance the wrong way simply because she wasn't tough enough to handle a man who, for some reason of his own, seemed determined to throw her off balance.

So she would grit her teeth and try very hard not to be hostile. Grit her teeth and try to smile. And think of her uncle.

'So where did you meet Alex?' he asked neutrally. She watched his hands slide over the coffee-pot and wondered, chaotically, what it would feel like to have his hands move so gently and so exploratively over her. 'It's cold,' he told her lightly, his mouth curling knowingly, exactly as if he could read her thoughts. 'Shall I ask Prinny to bring fresh?'

'Not for me.'

She sounded breathless. She shook her head to clear it and he sank down into the chair beside her, not opposite, as before, and prompted, 'Well?'

Fine brows peaked above golden eyes, and then she remembered. He had no right to question her, of course, and she had every right to refuse to tell him anything. Except that the wretch held her uncle's professional future in the palm of his hands

But how to answer?

Stick to the truth. She wasn't an easy liar. Thinking back quickly over the years, she told him, 'On a beach in Jamaica. I was fooling around in the water. Topless. I asked him to play with me.' Some inner devil made her add, 'How could he resist?' And she saw his eyes go bleak and hard, the tiny movement of a muscle at the side of his mouth. She had told him the truth and it was too bad if he didn't like it.

What she didn't tell him, had no intention of telling him, was that she'd been six years old at the time, splashing in and out of waves wearing a pair of navy blue knickers.

Her father had rented an old plantation house for three months, presumably to get to grips with the book of the moment. They'd been living out of suitcases for as long as she remembered. Having a settled home, for three whole months, had been quite an experience in her young life. And meeting her uncle and aunt for the first time, down there on that lonely beach, had been quite an experience, too.

Real family. Even at that tender age she had stopped thinking of her parents as family at all. They had always excluded her, her father wrapped up in his work, her mother wrapped up in him, perfectly content to hand her over like an unwanted package to whoever could be hired, or persuaded, to keep an eye on her for an hour, a day, or a week or two.

And her uncle and aunt had come halfway across the world to see her, tired of merely hearing about her in the scrappy and very occasional letters from her mother. It had made her feel beautifully important. And for four lovely weeks they had played with her, cuddled her, made sure she had proper meals at regular intervals, tucked her up in bed and told her stories until she fell asleep. For the first time in her young life she had felt she mattered to someone. When they had returned to England she had grieved.

And if the little she had told him merely served to reinforce his low opinion of her morals then what did she care?

But he said, his voice deceptively mild, 'Did it ever occur to you to keep yourself? You spend your life skimming around the world, from what I can gather. Yet you're highly intelligent, fluent in six languages——'

'Who the hell told you that?' She was appalled that he should know even that much about her. The fact that he knew anything at all made her feel threatened! Quite why that should be so she couldn't work out, and now wasn't the time to try, especially when he reached out for her hand, took it and turned it palm upwards as if trying to see her future in it.

'Alex, who else?' He gave her a glinting underbrow look and she snatched her hand away. So he'd been plying her uncle with questions as well as strong liquor while she'd been innocently freshening up. 'Does it matter? It's not a state secret, is it?'

'No, of course not,' she said stiffly, and got quickly to her feet. 'But what I do with my own life is my business.'

'It could be mine, too. Think about it while I walk you to your room.'

'How can I think about it, if I haven't the least idea what you're talking about?' she came back hoarsely, wishing quite hopelessly that she'd never allowed herself to get into this mess.

The house was utterly silent. Just the sound of their measured footsteps and the thunderous beat of her heart. She was quite sure he must be able to hear it and would put it down to raging sexual excitement, or something just as degrading. And he said softly, a smile in his voice, 'Of course you do.' His hand slipped round her waist as she stumbled on shamingly weak and unsteady legs at the top of the stairs. 'I've already said you intrigue me. And as I'm always honest, or at least I try to be, I'll admit that I want you.' His arm tightened around her waist as he swung her round, and the way his eyes probed hers, as if he could see something that was a secret even from herself, took her breath away. 'And if you'll stop pretending you don't feel the same we could begin to make progress.'

Fen was stunned, almost too dizzy to speak. But she forced herself, pushing at him with her hands bunched into fists.

'Stop mauling me! Is this how you get your women? No wonder none of them can stomach your company for more than a couple of days!'

For a moment he looked nonplussed and then he smiled grimly, subduing her useless struggles by wrapping his arms around her, his mouth a whisper away from hers as he murmured, 'Don't believe all the rumours you hear, Fen. You know nothing about my private life. But you will, you'll be part of it.' His voice thickened. His hands shaped her back, rising to her shoulders and down again, cupping her taut buttocks, scorching her skin through the silk of her dress. She was boneless and breathless, giddy and confused. She didn't know what was happening to her, why she should allow him such liberties. Quite probably, she thought wildly, she was going mad!

'Shall I show you how much you want to be part of my life, Fen?' His voice was a seduction in itself. She tried not to hear him but that was impossible. 'Shall I prove it to you, beyond any shadow of doubt?' His lips brushed hers. They were sweet, like honey, burning like a flame. She thought she was going to die. 'Shall I, Fen?'

She moaned thickly. He had relaxed his hold on her, his body brushing hers from her breasts to her thighs. It was torment. A sob of deep repudiation built up inside her, making her voice disgracefully thick as she managed, 'No! Don't!'

He thought she was easy, anybody's—providing the price was right! And the only way she could get herself out of this hateful mess was by telling him the truth, spelling out exactly how she and Alex had set out to get him back in the public eye, convince everyone that he wasn't a boring old has-been but a man in his prime, capable of attracting and holding female attention.

She had never liked the idea but never, in her wildest nightmares, could she have imagined it would rebound on her like this!

Just being seen with Alex at fashionable night-spots and restaurants would have been enough to boost his image and titillate the interest of female viewers. That was what Jean had said. And now look what had happened!

But she couldn't run the risk of explaining to Saul. He would believe, quite rightly, that he'd been made a fool of. And his monumental ego would demand revenge. Nothing would save Alex's programme if that happened!

And what would save her if she didn't? she thought wildly. The hateful man only had to touch her to take every last one of her senses by storm, to drive her customary cool composure deep underground and make her forget every single one of her firmly held principles.

He terrified her!

'You're quite right, Fen.' He released her, his hands sliding away slowly, with aching reluctance. 'Not with Alex under the same roof.' He made an abrupt, dismissive gesture with one hand. 'When I've squared it with him I'll move in for the kill.' The same hand lifted to trail slowly over her cheekbone to the corner of her mouth. His silver eyes gleamed, his lips curving wickedly. 'I'll make you admit you want me as much as I want you.'

Fen twisted her head away, her heart thundering mercilessly as she tried to armour her self-betraying senses against the silken threat of his touch, the things he was saying. And she saw him smile, intimately, as if they were sharing a delicious secret, her eyes going wide with something that was shamingly more than disbelief as he opened the door to the bedroom she'd been given, flicking on the lights and then walking away without another word.

Jerkily, she dived into the room and closed the door, locking it behind her. She was shaking all over, her breath coming in jagged, uneven gasps.

Relief, she told herself a little desperately. Just that. Relief that she had survived this evening relatively unscathed.

The man was a devil; she wouldn't be at all surprised if the elegant, hand-crafted leather shoes he wore covered cloven feet!

Normally, of course, she would have been able to handle him with as much cool indifference as she handled any man who tried to make a pass at her. Saul Ackerman wasn't in any way special, or different. And the fact that he had sent her haywire, made her experience sensations that were as previously unknown as they were unwanted, was nothing to do with him personally. It was the situation that was out of the normal, the games she and Alex had been playing, her inability to put him straight about her morals—or supposed lack of them—without landing her uncle in the soup. That was why the loathsome Saul Ackerman had been able to shake her composure. Nothing else.

'We have to leave. Right now, Alex,' Fen hissed into her uncle's ashen face as she smartly exited her room. 'If Mrs Pringle offers you breakfast, refuse.'

At the mention of breakfast Alex's face turned a delicate shade of green but he did manage, 'But Saul— I can't just walk out without——'

'He left hours ago,' Fen said tightly, wishing her uncle could make himself move just a little faster than a geriatric snail. She was sure their host had left just before nine. She'd been awake for hours, her ears straining until they ached. She'd heard firm, decisive steps moving down the corridor outside her room at around eight and three-quarters of an hour later the sound of a car engine, tyres scattering gravel on the drive. And then the drone of vacuum cleaners, then nothing until those slow, shambling steps approaching her room.

And who knew when Saul was due back? She couldn't face him. She wouldn't face him! As far as he was concerned it was a case of out of sight, out of mind. And the sooner they were off his premises, the sooner she would be able to forget his very existence.

'I'll drive,' she asserted firmly as she chivvied Alex down the stairs and out into the sunlight. He groaned and screwed his eyes shut against the glare but Fen growled, 'If you don't hurry I'll leave you here and you can darned well walk home!' treating him like a naughty child because she could be tougher and more determined than most when it was a matter of her survival.

And although she wasn't prepared to question herself too closely she knew that her survival depended on never seeing Saul Ackerman again!

CHAPTER FIVE

TOMORROW couldn't come soon enough!

Fen finished the dusting and mooched through into the kitchen to make coffee, wondering whether to spend the day in town or simply curl up with a good book.

Apart from being an ancient market town nestling comfortably beneath the frowning mass of Dartmoor, with a history stretching back a thousand years, Tavistock, as she knew, had a fine covered pannier market where one could buy anything from a cushion to a cod fish and, even more temptingly, there was a newly opened and exceptionally good boutique, or so Jean had told her. And Fen itched to go shopping. She always did when she was miserable or on edge. Other women might munch through pounds of chocolate, or fall on the gin bottle; she went shopping.

But she couldn't really afford to indulge herself, not and stay solvent, and her next job wasn't until the end of June when she was due in Milan to translate a book of children's modern fables into English for an Italian publishing company. The trouble with accepting only work she really enjoyed was the occasional shortage of funds. Which could mean that if she didn't harbour her resources she might have to take on a stint of private language tuition, her least favourite means of earning her bread because it meant staying put for longer than she was comfortable with, she thought gloomily as she waited for the kettle to boil.

So shopping was out. And in any case, there was no reason on earth why she should feel despondent and edgy, was there? She and Alex between them had sorted everything out.

She'd been very near to panic when she'd driven her uncle away from Saul Ackerman's home yesterday. She who never panicked, who took life and turned it into something that suited her, who did her own thing and was accountable to no one, panicking because a man had said he wanted her! She dismayed herself!

She would have preferred to drive through the afternoon to reach the relative safety of Hampstead. But Alex, slumped in the passenger seat had groaned pathetically, 'Not Hampstead. I can't sit in the car for hours. We'll stay in Tavi. God, I made a fool of myself last night! He'll think I'm a lush. Did he say anything to you? No—don't tell me! I need to get back to bed. And quick. It'll be a week before I feel human again!'

So the Tavistock house it had been, and was, and Alex's dire prognosis had proved incorrect because when he'd come down to breakfast this morning he'd looked perfectly human again, his heavy eyes the only sign of his unaccustomed drinking session.

'Am I forgiven?' He'd accepted his toast and coffee with chastened gratitude.

'Of course. You're entitled to kick over the traces once in a while. But I've been thinking...' She had been, all night, or so it seemed. 'I don't believe there's any point in our going back to Town again and haunting the fashionable night-spots on the off-chance we'll be photographed together. I know we said we'd give it a couple of weeks before I slid off the face of the earth and you went back to Jean. But——'

'I know.' He cut her short and patted her hand across the breakfast-table. 'You never liked the idea, but once you'd agreed you threw yourself whole-heartedly into the part and for that alone Jean and I will always be grateful. And I agree with you. I've no stomach for it now, either. And, whatever decision is reached regarding my future with VisionWest, more scandalous publicity isn't going to make a jot of difference.' He swallowed his orange juice and then his coffee and poured himself another of both, looking better by the second. 'I'll drive into Plymouth this morning; I've an idea there's a board meeting and there's a chance Saul will be there. I need to see him and apologise for my lapse and the way we left without so much as a thank-you. I'd offer to take you along, too, but I don't think it would be wise. From the way he was questioning me about you the other evening I've got the feeling his interest is more than merely academic. I told him as little as I could, of course, without seeming to snub him. But the less you see of him the better, I think.'

He was getting ready to leave, pulling on his suit jacket and patting his pockets to find his car keys. And Fen went very still, a shiver icing its way down her spine.

'What do you mean?' Her voice came out sounding tinny.

Alex shook his head at her wryly.

'It's not hard to tell when a man fancies a woman, Fen, only you're such an innocent, you probably wouldn't have picked it up. And despite his looks, not to mention all that wealth and power, a fling with him is not what I'd prescribe for you. He's tough and he's bitter. Not the type I want around my little girl.'

'And never seen with the same woman twice,' Fen supplied stiffly, feeling sick inside.

A relative innocent she might be when it came to intimate relationships with the opposite sex, but Saul had left her in no doubt at all that he wanted her and meant to have her.

But she couldn't tell Alex that. He was as protective of her as if she had been his own daughter and he would go straight to Saul and admit the deception, tell him that his niece was not that kind of woman, was not the type to indulge in lustful flings between the sheets with any man who cared to ask. And in doing so he would make Saul feel a fool, an importuning fool, and could wave any hopes of a renewed contract away. So she would cope with it on her own, make herself scarce until Alex had received the decision the director of programmes had promised. And she wasn't really listening when Alex answered her.

'That's more or less true. But it doesn't mean he's sleeping with them. He keeps his private life to himself. Even when his marriage was breaking up he didn't betray a thing. And on the day after his wife died he was back in harness as if nothing had happened.'

Then, seeing the sudden, stinging attention, the stunned pallor of her face, he shrugged. 'That's hearsay, of course. I'd never met him until the consortium he headed won the franchise. But it comes from a reliable source.' He smiled, attempting to lighten the atmosphere. 'Not that it matters. You're not likely to see him again. And even if you did, forewarned is forearmed, as they say. So.' He straightened his tie. 'What are you going to do with yourself today?'

His wife was dead and he hadn't blinked an eye! What had she died of? A broken heart and disillusionment? He was more than a sex-mad bastard—he was evil! Gathering herself, Fen began to stack the used breakfast china, forcing herself to answer lightly, 'I'll get my things together—I'll pick up the stuff I left at Hampstead in a week or two—and hire a car. I thought I'd go down to the cottage and clear it out, ready to put it on the market. I'll drive down tomorrow.'

Out of that devil's way. Always presuming he'd meant what he'd said about squaring things with Alex to leave the way clear for him to show her how much she wanted him! The ratfink! The evil, callous louse!

'No need to hire a car, Fen. Save your money. I'll drive you down. A couple of days on the coast sounds good to me, too. I'll sort out any business at the studios and then we can both lie low. I'll give you a hand at the cottage, see you're properly provisioned and drive up to Edinburgh until Jean's ready to come back. We'll both come down and pick you up when you're ready to leave.'

So no, she couldn't wait until tomorrow.

She stared broodingly at the mug of coffee on the work surface. She didn't want it, so why had she made it? Then the phone rang and she went through to the sitting-room to answer it, relieved because she had something to do. It was probably Jean and they could have a nice long natter. But dismay sent her stomach plummeting down to her shoes and back up into her throat as Saul Ackerman said, 'I need to see you. I'll pick you up at eight this evening and give you dinner. It's up to you whether you tell Alex where you'll be.'

'No.' She snapped the word out without having to think about it at all. His arrogance took her breath away. She would have slammed the receiver down because just hearing him speak put her in turmoil, but he said quietly, 'I have something to discuss with you, regarding Alex and his future with VisionWest, and I refuse to do it over the phone. Eight o'clock.'

'No.' But this time not quite so decisively. He was threatening Alex's future, through her. She didn't have the right to refuse to listen to him, regardless. Not when it was her uncle who would have to pay the price. But dinner? Probably not here in Tavistock, either, but in the more intimate setting of his lovely home. 'Lunch,' she temporised.

'If you say so.' He sounded faintly amused, as if he had been tuned in to the thoughts that had scurried through her brain, and she pushed in warily.

'And not at your home, either.' She couldn't stand to be alone with him there. He shouldn't be allowed to live in such a breathtakingly lovely place. It was like plucking a perfect blossom and finding a hairy black spider deep in the heart of the scented petals.

'Scared, Fen?' She could hear him smiling, damn him! 'Don't be. I'll pick you up in a couple of hours.'

Which would make it around one o'clock, she thought as the line went dead. She wiped her sweaty palms down the sides of her jeans. There was no need to feel quite so nervous. He couldn't make her do a thing she didn't want to do.

But telling herself that didn't help because he had already forced her to agree to have lunch with him! Groaning, she wondered whether she should use the next couple of hours shopping for something for supper. There was nothing in the fridge. But she felt far too unsettled to concentrate on buying meat and vegetables. Besides, her hair was a mess and needed washing, and she had to ferret out something suitably restrained to wear...

She didn't have a lot of choice but she eventually settled for black leggings topped by a loose-fitting, silky black T-shirt that came down to her thighs. She looked, she congratulated herself, like a beanpole. And the spiky black heels she was wearing merely emphasised the effect. Not even the sex-mad Saul Ackerman could find a black beanpole alluring!

Not bothering with make-up—just a hint of copper-toned lipstick—she flicked a comb through her newly washed hair, the thick golden fringe bouncing against her eyebrows. Then she was as ready as she would ever be for the coming ordeal.

But, as the fingers of the clock in the guest room moved nearer to one, her heart began to hammer against her breastbone, her stomach tying itself in knots. And she knew she wouldn't have been quite this nervous if he hadn't told her not to be! She didn't trust him, with very good reason. And although she had no idea what he wanted to discuss—or only loosely in that it was to do with Alex's professional future—she tried to comfort herself with the thought that there was very little he could do to her over a lunch table, in full view of all the other people around.

But even that small solace was denied her when the imperious ring of the doorbell had her stalking fatalistically down the stairs. He handed her into the sleekly expensive perfection of his car and gestured to a tote bag on the back seat.

'I had Prinny pack us a picnic. I thought we'd go up to the edge of the moors.' And he whisked her away before she could begin to object.

Slumping in her seat, Fen wondered when luck would start running with her, instead of against her. The way he looked didn't help, either. A soft-as-butter fawn leather jacket covered a black T-shirt and snug-fitting black denims. The formal authority of the hard-eyed business giant had been sloughed off along with his impeccable formal suits, making him appear younger, more approachable. Someone she could relate to. Like. Like?

Utter nonsense! How could she ever come near to liking such a man? A man who hadn't turned a hair when his wife died. Even if their marriage had been on the rocks he should have felt some grief and regret.

She slanted him a withering sideways glare and caught her breath. It was still there, all right; all the authority in the world was stamped on that austerely impressive profile. How could she have imagined that the casual clothes could make a scrap of difference?

She looked away quickly, not seeing anything through the window at her side, brooding darkly to herself as he negotiated Tavistock's one-way system. And only when they were heading for the open road did she negotiate a shaky way through the atmosphere of unbelievably forceful awareness that smouldered between them in the intimate confines of the car by muttering at him, 'I'm not dressed for tramping on the moors. And I'm not hungry, either. So why don't you pull into the next lay-by and tell me what this is all in aid of?' She had no intention of spending the long afternoon with him on the empty moors, with only the silent and vaguely sinister standing stones to keep them company, the great purple masses of the high moors crowding against the skyline, shutting her in. With him.

Fen shuddered with chilling remembrance.

She'd been fourteen and too adventurous for her own good. Six years before, when she'd been around eight, her parents had bought the cottage on the Cornish coast, west of Polperro, largely, she believed, because Alex and Jean had hounded them into having somewhere that could loosely be called a home base, for her sake.

Until she'd finally cut loose from her parents, able to fend for herself, she had spent several weeks each summer there. Sometimes her parents had come along, too, and sometimes not. It depended on whether her father could tear himself away from wherever he happened to be on the planet. But Alex and Jean had always been there, without fail, and they'd made it a family holiday, reinforcing the bonds that had been forged on that beach in Jamaica.

But for a few weeks of the summer when she was fourteen they'd all been there together. The atmosphere between her and her parents hadn't been good. In fact it had been rotten, with her father laying the law down and her mother backing him up and Fen alternatively raging or sulking.

They had decided she was to spend the next two years in an English boarding-school, spending her holidays with Alex and Jean. Fen hadn't objected to that part. But boarding-school? Staying in one place for two whole years?

Moving from place to place with her parents, from country to country as her father researched his travel books, had become her way of life. Attending local schools wherever they happened to be, picking up languages with no trouble at all, she had never known any thing else and the foundations had been well and truly laid for a footloose existence. She would never put down roots, and certainly not in an English boarding-school!

Out of humour with the whole world—even the people she loved most in the world, Alex and Jean, had been on her parents' side—she had taken the bike she kept in the shed and had set off at dawn for the moors. Bodmin Moor.

She hadn't bothered to check the weather forecast or take extra clothing. All she'd been interested in was a day of freedom, away from the adults who seemed set on making her do the thing she least wanted to do. But freedom had turned into a prison when the mist had come down, disorientating her, turning Bodmin into a vast tract of isolation and danger.

It had been long, cold, miserable hours later before she had stumbled on to a deserted and definitely minor road, more by luck than by judgement. Too exhausted even to think of tackling the long ride home, she had trudged on until she'd stumbled across a roadside cottage where she'd begged the use of a phone.

It had been Jean who had fetched her in the Land Rover, complete with blankets and forceful remonstrances. Didn't she know how foolhardy it was to go so far on her own? Bodmin, too! Even if by the time she'd cycled there she hadn't had the energy to penetrate much beyond the edges of all that wildness, it had been a stupid thing to do! Didn't she care that they had all been worried witless because she'd been missing all day, leaving no clue to where she might have gone?

'You're fourteen years old and capable of making your own decisions—or so you keep telling us!' Jean had remarked sternly. 'Yet you behaved with about as much common sense as a four-year-old today. Don't you think the adults who care about you know what's best for your future?'

Fen had known what she was talking about, of course. That wretched boarding-school. And although she had doubts about her parents, she knew Alex and Jean loved her and cared about her future. So, on that day, she had given in, accepted parental dictates. And, amazingly, hadn't regretted it.

But she had been left with a fear of the moors. And the Devon moors would be much the same as the Cornish Bodmin. And because Saul had ignored her request that they stop at the next lay-by to discuss whatever it was he wanted to say she repeated, 'I don't fancy a moorland hike and a cheese buttie. Please pull in to the side of the road.'

'Any time now,' he promised soothingly.

A sneaked sideways glance revealed the amused quirk of his mouth. She'd been right he was laughing at her. Finding her strictures funny because he had every intention of doing exactly as he pleased, and planned. Regardless. She shuddered, and put the reaction down to memories of another time, another moor.

But Dartmoor today was smiling, rolling green and gold beneath the endless soft blue sky and Saul eased the car off the road and on to a narrower, stony track, then, where the track dipped, off on to the short, springy grass, and cut the engine, turning to her.

'The best of both worlds—just for you. The benefits of the view and the air without having to walk more than a yard on your four-inch heels.'

Twisting her reasons for objecting to the outing. He had to know she wouldn't willingly share a thing with him—a view, a picnic, whatever.

He was a manipulator, almost too self-assured to be believable, and the only way she could hope to combat him was to stay exactly where she was, glued to the leather upholstery, until he recognised the futility of having brought her here and headed back to Tavistock.

But now that the car was stationary it was impossible to stay cooped up inside with him. Impossible. The smouldering awareness was growing, assuming terrifying proportions. With a soft anguished gasp she reached for the door release and scrambled out, taut as a bowstring as the early summer sun stroked her tense body, pulling in steadying breaths while she waited for him to join her.

'Couldn't be more tranquil, could it?' He came to stand beside her, carrying a soft woollen blanket and the bag. Even wearing her highest heels the top of her head only reached a fraction above the level of his wide, rangy shoulders. She took a teetering step away, her breath coming raggedly despite all her attempts to stay calm and in control. Was he trying to impress their isolation on her? Only a few hundred yards away from the road she knew was back there somewhere, they might as well be alone in the great sprawling loneliness of the moors. He had no need to hammer home the obvious!

'You said you had something to discuss,' she pointed out, turning away as he draped the rug on the ground and shrugged out of his leather jacket. The soft black T-shirt clung altogether too lovingly to his impressive torso. He was in peak condition, superbly fit. She couldn't look!

'So I have. But let's be civilised about it, and eat first.' She felt his eyes on her and shivered.

She wouldn't be able to eat a thing, but the more she tried to push him into telling her what he had wanted to talk to her about, the more he would resist.

Just for the hell of it, just to let her know he was in charge. Now and always.

No, not always, she contradicted herself. Only until Alex's future with VisionWest had been decided. When Laurence Meek had made his decision Saul Ackerman wouldn't see her for dust!

Grudgingly, she sat on the very edge of the rug, staring into the distance, and he said softly, 'I don't bite, Fen. Or only when provoked.'

She shot him an unguarded look from beneath her fringe and met that mocking, slanting smile, felt the power of those silver eyes latch on to her own and couldn't look away, not even when he added warningly, 'So try not to provoke me. At least, not until we've eaten.'

'I...' Her voice was too thick, her mouth too dry. She couldn't get a word out, couldn't look away. Did he fascinate every woman he met...? Did he have that much power...?

'Drink this.' He put a can of Coke into her nerveless hands, dealing with the ring-pull for her, his fingers touching hers, scorching them. Fen pulled away, her golden eyes mirroring panic, and his smile was carelessly amused although, she noted shakily, his eyes were speculative.

She moistened her lips with the tip of her tongue, desperate to find the words that would make him understand he didn't impress her, or scare her. But nothing would come and she lifted the can to her mouth, hiding her hopeless inadequacy, unable to murmur even the smallest acknowledgement when he

handed her a fat Cornish pastie wrapped in a heavy
linen napkin.

She had made a scathing reference to cheese butties
but privately had expected his offering to be more of
the caviare and champagne variety. But the simple,
wholesome food was not going to make her change
any of her denigrating opinions of him.

But she did begin to relax, just a little, helped by
a cheery greeting from a group of hikers who came
down the track, heavy boots clattering on the stones.
She watched them tramp away, and even when they
had disappeared into the distance she no longer felt
quite so isolated, relaxed enough now to draw her
knees up to her chin and squint sideways at Saul as
he flopped down full-length on his side, propping his
dark head up on one curving hand.

'Do you have any deep feelings for Alex at all?'
Asked with impeccable politeness, his question took
her breath away. Just for a moment she had been beginning to unwind, enjoy the play of the soft warm
air on her face, the silence which had, to her retro-
spective astonishment, turned companionable and
easy.

How to answer? Truthfully, or in character? Bearing
in mind the scandalous lies she and her uncle had
planted inside Saul's head, and the fact that after tomorrow the so-called affair would be over, with Alex
going to Edinburgh to be with Jean once he had helped
her settle in at the cottage, proving to Joe Public that
his heart belonged to his wife, and no one else, Fen
opted for answering in character.

'He's quite a guy. Great fun, and sexy with it.' The words tasted foul in her mouth, and she couldn't look at him. If their so-called affair was supposed to be a thing of small substance, as it must be if he were to 'return' to his wife after so short a fling, then she couldn't admit to more.

It was an utterly hateful situation to be in! And made doubly so when Saul said, a tinge of deep disgust in his voice, 'He's much too old for you. But I suppose that doesn't matter to you, so long as he can show you a good time and pay the bills.'

'You're disgusting!' Fen rounded on him furiously, remembering, too late, that she and Alex, aided by the gutter Press, had put that idea in his head. He wasn't to blame, they were!

Her eyes fell, thrown into confusion by the derisory gleam in that clever silver gaze. And she mumbled, dropping her chin to her knees again and sheltering her bright head with her arms, 'It's not like that. You can't begin to understand.' And that was the truth, but feeble. Why wasn't she telling him to mind his own damn business? Why wasn't she stalking back to the car with her head held high, demanding to be taken back to town?

Suddenly, Fen didn't understand herself at all and it made her feel confused and miserable; there was a wretched lump in her throat, forbidding any hope of vocal reaction, when he said softly, 'Then make me understand, Fen. Tell me how it is.'

She simply shook her buried head, her eyes tightly closed against her leggings-clad knees, and when she felt the brush of his fingers against the exposed and vulnerable nape of her neck she went into shock.

It had to be shock; nothing else could explain why she endured his touch. Endured the caress that found the sensitive hollow behind her ear and slid down the fragile curve of her neck to tuck in beneath the neckline of her T-shirt. Shock that set up the quivering chain reaction inside her, holding her weak and immobile, then making her gasp as his arms snaked around her, pulling her down on to the rug beside him, keeping her there by the power of the ruthless need she saw glinting in his eyes.

Fighting back shameful excitement, she said huskily, 'Let me go, damn you!' and saw his mouth curl in a tight feral smile as he answered with dark menace,

'Only when you really want me to.' And he slid his hand beneath the hem of her T-shirt, gliding upwards to close possessively over one firmly peaked naked breast and then its twin, his thumb rolling tellingly over her revealingly taut nipples, his actions making her fully understand where his words had failed.

Fen moaned, her mind in anguish. That decidedly independent mind of hers rebelled at the thought of his effortless sexual domination. But, with his own special brand of dark, masculine magic, he made her female body crave to surrender to his potency.

'Don't fight it, Fen,' he murmured, those silver eyes heavy-lidded now with desire. His hand smoothed a honeyed track down over the soft swell of her stomach, which feathered with a treachery that matched the traitorous need deep inside her beneath the waistband of her leggings. 'You want me; your body gives you away. Tell me you don't and you'll be telling me you're a liar.'

'No!'

Her head thrashed heavily, spilling bright hair against the soft dark wool of the rug, her body alive with shaming pleasure, her breath rushing out of her lungs as he brought his dark head down to hers, his mouth a statement of male sensuality, his kiss a foregone conclusion as he whispered heavily, 'Don't turn a simple physical attraction into a three-act drama, Fen. There's no problem. Leave Alex and come to me.'

CHAPTER SIX

THE kiss seemed to go on forever. It was the only reality. Fen was breathless and giddy and the more thoroughly Saul kissed her, the more her lips clung to his, aching for their repossession when he briefly lifted his head, inviting her, or so it seemed, to drown in the slumbrous depths of his suddenly darkened eyes.

There was, she recognised with a tiny gasp, complete physical rapport between then, a drugging sensation of oneness that made her whole body ache for his possession. Madness, but a magical madness that had nothing to do with logic. Her fingers tightened on his shoulders, digging into hard muscle and bone, and he dipped his head, reading her message, and her eyelids fluttered down on a sigh as his mouth brushed hers, tantalising, teasing, opening her lips and sipping at the inner sweetness.

She had never felt like this before, weak and filled with wickedly desirous sensation, clinging to him as if he were the only reality in her universe. Nothing had prepared her for this. Nothing. Certainly not Ray's clumsy lovemaking. That had left her feeling nothing but embarrassment and distaste, leavened just briefly with regret, a hint of sadness, because all that talk of love, of the physical wonder that could exist between a man and a woman, was nothing but a fable, designed to trap the gullible and insecure into forming a contract that would ensure the survival of the species.

But this magic, this need . . . ?

'Can you lie to me now?' he asked thickly, slowly breaking the kiss, and she shuddered, clinging on to him weakly, not understanding, not yet. 'Face the truth. You want me as I want you. The moment we met, our bodies knew. There can be only one outcome, Fen. Admit it.'

'Oh, God . . .' It was like the voice of a drugged woman, or a dying woman. And his eyes were eyes you could drown in, soft and hazy and deep. The austere lines of his face were gentler, his slashing mouth warm now with passion, and her pulses leapt with response, hammering wildly as she belatedly fought against his sexual domination, fought to find her lost reason.

'Leave me be!' She twisted away from him, all the determination she was capable of injected into that one writhing movement.

He was a devil! He had reached into her psyche and discovered all that latent sensuality. She had been blissfully unaware of it herself but one look, apparently, had led him straight to its simmering core. He had picked up vibrations she hadn't known were there. It was dark magic, a knowledge he had reaped with one look from those clever eyes, gathered and used to trap her.

It couldn't be endured!

She scrambled to her feet, tugging her T-shirt back in place, her breath coming in painful gasps. But he was right there with her, his big body brushing hers, his voice husky with amused determination as he asked her, 'Why? Why fight the fascination?'

Fascination. Was that what it was? Her eyes darkened to topaz. Had she in her ceaseless search for all the reasons she should hate and despise him been covering up the fact that she'd found him fascinating from the moment she'd first set eyes on him? Oh, dear God, was that what all those protestations had been about?

She was beginning to think she didn't know herself at all, and she was beginning to shake. He placed his hands on her shoulders, his thumbs gently rotating against the curve above her collarbone. And if he thought he was preventing her from stalking away, then he was mistaken. The leashed strength of his hands wasn't stopping her. He held her within his dark thraldom. She couldn't have moved if her life had depended on it.

'Give me one good reason why you shouldn't move in with me.' Warm sunlight drew chestnut glints from the dark thickness of his hair, highlighted the pure silver that gleamed through curling dark lashes and emphasised the passionate curve of his mouth. Fen shuddered, fighting the instinct to lean into his body, curve her arms around his neck and let principles go hang.

But she knew what he meant and, what was worse, what he thought. She was the type of woman who sold herself to the highest bidder, preferring to live off a man rather than tie herself down to a routine job. Footloose and fickle, trading on her looks. She was trapped in the web of deceit she, Alex and Jean had woven.

There was only one way to go, even if it did mean she would be digging the pit of deception deeper with her own tongue. She had to take it because she couldn't tell him the truth, not yet. And she wouldn't have an affair with him, even if she had wanted to—which, she hastily assured herself, she didn't—not while he thought she was nothing more than a high-class tramp!

'Alex,' she said, forcing speech through stiff lips, 'is reason enough.'

She felt his body stiffen. And although his mouth was still smiling his eyes went hard.

'Such loyalty. I'm impressed. It's rare, in my experience.' He was no longer smiling and his hands dropped from her shoulders, his mouth twisting in curling contempt as he bit out, 'What about the loyalty Alex owes to his wife? Or doesn't that count? If you have any feelings for him at all you'll tell him goodbye, send him back to Jean with his tail between his legs. He'll go of his own accord sooner or later.'

'So you keep telling me,' she flung back acidly. Two could be bitter and twisted; he hadn't cornered the market on contempt, either, and she tacked on, 'Would you be so desperate to see them reunited if you didn't want to take me away from him and install me in your bed?'

'Probably not.'

Her eyes flickered and fell beneath the shock of his honesty, and even without looking at him she could sense the change, feel the ebbing of tension as he gathered himself to soften her up for the kill.

She wasn't going to give him that opportunity and stumbled stiff-leggedly away, back to the car, and he followed her, slowly yet remorselessly, and he pinned her with cold, ungenerous eyes, all the abrasiveness back in his voice as he explained, 'As you won't listen to what your senses tell you, or to simple logic, let me put it another way. I'm free, Alex isn't. Sooner or later he'll go back to his wife and you will have to start looking for another man to pay the bills. You might not find one. You might even have to start working to buy your bread. Move in with me and you won't have to look. And in case you should feel guilty about giving him the push, don't be. I'll throw in a cast-iron contract for him as my side of the bargain.'

'That's blackmail!' she scorned, and leant weakly against the gleaming bodywork of the car. Her eyes glittered suddenly with tears and she blinked them furiously away, her breath catching in her throat as he admitted smoothly,

'Exactly.'

'But you don't even like me!' she wailed, confused by his calmness, the way he opened the car and tossed the rug and the bag that had held their lunch on to the back seat, not even looking at her now, not trying to persuade her with the dark power of his physical persuasion.

'So?' A black brow drifted upwards in cool derision. 'How can I like someone I can't respect? That's the one thing I can't give you.' He held the door open, waiting for her to get into the passenger seat but she stood where she was, the shock of the insult making her feel as if she'd just been flattened by a ten-ton truck.

Wildly, her eyes searched his features, looking in vain for some hint of redeeming sanity behind his motivations. And when he added drily, 'However, I am sure you will find compensations,' her sense of outrage was complete and she slid her long legs into the car and informed him haughtily,

'Don't bank on it. You may be used to buying your women—it's probably the only way you can get them. But I can't, and won't, be bought. Or blackmailed. And if you ever manage to grow a heart, ever begin to understand that there's more to a relationship than a quick tumble, give me a call and I'll see if I'm available.'

And that, she decided with a strange dredging sensation around the region of her heart, was that. Judging by the thick black silence as he drove back to town, he would never even contemplate having anything to do with her ever again.

'Now, you're sure you'll be all right? You've got everything you need?'

'Of course I'm sure.' She had space and freedom and solitude, which was all her muddled mind craved at the moment. Fen leaned forward to kiss her uncle's cheek, moving back from the open car window as he started the engine. 'Drive carefully. And be sure to make an overnight stop—no trying to drive to Scotland in one go!'

He grinned at her. 'We'll phone you in a couple of weeks, when we're back in Tavi. And we'll come and fetch you just as soon as you've finished here.' And then he was gone, the car bumping up the precipitous, narrow lane which had grass growing all down the middle and big shaggy hedgerows that encroached on either side.

They had been at the cottage for the best part of two days and he couldn't wait to get to Edinburgh to be with Jean. They had missed each other dreadfully. Although childless, theirs was a marriage many would envy. The exception rather than the rule, Fen dismissed too easily as she waved him out of sight.

Frowning, she kicked a pebble along the dusty track and stuffed her hands into the pockets of her jeans. Although her uncle had tried not to let it show, she knew he'd been worried about the renewal of his contract. Saul hadn't attended that board meeting, he'd confided, so he hadn't been able to have a word with him and convey his apologies for the way they'd driven away from his home without so much as a thank-you. But he'd left a note with his secretary, and hoped that would suffice.

And Fen hadn't had the nerve to tell him that she knew Saul had absented himself from that meeting, and why. That he had spent the time with her, trying to persuade her to become his mistress, offering a cast-iron contract for Alex as an extra inducement. And how could she possibly confess that the scathing things she'd said to Saul meant that a renewed contract was about the last thing Alex could look for?

It was all down to this fatal fascination, she brooded. If Saul hadn't seen her with Alex and—and lusted after her, believing her to be some sort of career-mistress who could be bought, provided the price and conditions were right, then none of this would have happened.

If he had simply seen her with Alex, read the scandalous reports in the Press—and hadn't fancied her himself and got all male and rampant about it—then he would have just shrugged it off, believing Alex was not such a dull old stick as his ratings seemed to confirm, watched the ensuing publicity for the 'old has-been' with those cold, cynical eyes, and everything would have gone the way they'd planned it.

And she wouldn't have been affected, wouldn't have discovered that she could respond so blindly, with such wild, instinctive passion to a man's touch. She would have continued to walk happily through her independent life, relying on no one but herself for a single damn thing. But now...

But nothing!

Firming her mouth, Fen sliced all thoughts of Saul Ackerman, of what he had done to her and the way he had made her feel, right out of her mind and pushed open the wicket gate set in the overgrown escallonia hedge that surrounded the tiny garden and breathed in the scented, salt-tanged, sun-warmed early morning air. She had a job to do and she was going to get on with it.

The stone cottage was built low, backed into the green hillside for shelter, huddling beneath its sturdy slate roof, and looking down on the small rocky cove where once the local people had wrested a living of sorts from the sea. The tiny village itself was a scant half a mile away, up the steep narrow track, taking advantage of the shelter of the gentle, wooded hills and hidden from view. The only indication that it was there was the odd plume of smoke from some of the chimneys, curling up through the trees.

In a way it would be a pity to see the cottage sold, she thought as she pushed open the front door and stepped on to the great slabs of granite that covered the entire ground floor. She had spent some wonderful weeks in summer here as a child with her uncle and aunt. Those holidays had been the one constant in her younger years, the cottage the only place that had ever come near to resembling a permanent home.

But no one had come near it during the last couple of years except Jean and Alex, who had driven down from time to time to check on it. Her mother would never come again and she, Fen, had no use for a base. Besides, she couldn't afford to buy it from her mother.

During the past couple of days she and Alex had aired the little house, flinging the windows wide and sweeping out the worst of the accumulation of dust. And they had stocked up with enough provisions to last for at least two weeks. If she ran short of anything she only had to clamber up the lane to the village. So she had nothing to distract her from the task in hand.

At the head of the twisty, uncarpeted stairs she walked into the room she had chosen to use during her stay here. As a child she had been consigned to the box room, little bigger than a cupboard, while

Jean and Alex had had what had been grandly termed the guest room. This room had been used by her parents whenever they had decided to spend time with her here during those long-ago summers, and even now she felt an interloper.

But that was nothing to get maudlin about. It was nothing new. She had always felt an interloper in her parents' lives. What she should be getting depressed about right now was the heap of classy carriers stacked guiltily at the bottom of the old-fashioned wardrobe!

When Saul had dropped her off in the centre of Tavistock, at her terse request, she'd had nothing more in mind than a quick trip to the market to buy fish for supper. Only somehow she'd got side-tracked and had ended up in the boutique Jean had told her about, and, her state of mind being what it was after what had happened up there on the moors, she had predictably gone on a wild spending spree. Her bank account would be empty and she would have to hunt around for a private tuition job.

And it was all Saul Ackerman's fault! If he hadn't got her into such a turmoil she wouldn't have succumbed to the panacea of impulse shopping. He ought to be shot!

Muttering to herself, and still too guilty even to think of unpacking those carriers, she stuck her head in a dusty cupboard and began to sort through her father's books and papers.

Unknown hours later, she was still at it, the things she knew her mother would want kept stacked in a neat pile on the floor, ready to be taken back to Tavistock to be carefully packed for the long overseas journey, the rubbish pushed into a bin bag. And this was only the start of it.

Wearily, Fen pushed her dusty fingers through her fringe and sat back on her heels, frowning just a little as the oncoming sound of a car engine broke the drowsy afternoon silence.

Not a local, for sure. If the villagers came down to the cove they came on foot, although they rarely did, seeming to prefer the busier delights of Polperro or Looe. So it had to be a car full of holiday-makers, though they were rare in this quiet area. Few of them ventured through the winding tangle of narrow lanes to the village above, and the precipitous track leading down to the tiny cove was enough to put anyone off.

Not giving the hapless adventurers another thought, she got stiffly to her feet and tried to ease her aching back. It was time for a break. Her throat was parched. And she was halfway down the stairs when she registered the silence again. The car had stopped. Or backed away up the track. Then she sighed resignedly as someone pounded heavily against the door.

Lost. Looking for directions. Or, as had once happened, asking if they could get a cup of tea. And whoever it was they needn't sound so irate about it. It wasn't her fault they'd landed up at the back of beyond instead of in some bustling holiday centre!

'I'm coming,' she muttered under her breath as the pounding began again, and tried not to scowl as she covered the distance to the door in a few long strides and pulled it open. The Cornish were known for their friendly hospitality and she didn't want to let her adopted county down by appearing to be anything less.

But her hastily assumed friendly smile died the death when she saw who was filling her doorstep, his elegantly cut business suit and gleaming handmade leather shoes looking totally out of place against the backdrop of exuberant escallonia.

'You!' Fen knew she sounded as if she was being strangled, but couldn't help it. After the things she had said to him she had never expected to see him again. But whether she had secretly hoped to see him again was brought into question by the way her heart wrenched painfully inside her, her pulses pounding out a wild drumbeat that made her gasp for breath, made her toes curl in her sensible canvas shoes.

He gave her a cool look, his features frozen. And his voice was pure ice as he drawled, 'So Alex learned some sense and decided to conduct his affair out of the limelight.' His narrowed eyes pierced the interior of the cottage. 'Secluded—even for a love-nest. Where is he?' He clipped the question out, almost rocking her back on her heels, and when she'd recovered she dragged in a very firm breath and set her mouth in a straight, ungiving line.

How could she have wondered if she had secretly been hoping to see him again? He was nothing but a waste of space as far as she was concerned.

Alex had once told her of an ancient Cornish saying, that the devil never ventured to cross the Tamar from England into Cornwall for fear of being caught and put in a Cornish pastie. Well, they'd been wrong. The devil was here, on her doorstep! And if she had her way she would make him into mincemeat!

'Well? he prompted impatiently, his brows thundering together in the face of her obduracy. 'Where is he?'

'Not here.' Her response was as clipped and cool as she could make it but her voice fractured as he brushed past her, striding into the living area and glaring around as if he expected to find Alex cowering behind one of the shabby but comfortable, overstuffed armchairs.

'You can't just barge into my home without so much as a by-your-leave!' Being around him was giving her lots of practice when it came to huffing and puffing she thought, half hysterically, as she noted the way one strongly marked brow drifted elegantly towards his hairline. She braced herself to receive his scathing comment.

'So he set you up here, did he? Got the deeds safely stashed away, have you?' Cool eyes raked over the homey surroundings, the stack of logs Alex had carried in yesterday and piled up for her beside the open fireplace. 'I'd have thought a penthouse apartment in the glitter of big-city lights would have been more to your taste. But I can see the attraction of complete isolation—from his point of view.'

Fen had had more than enough. True, she had given him every reason to believe she was no better than she should be, but was there any need for him to insult her so often and so heavily? It was, she decided, pulling herself up to her not insignificant height, high time she put him right on one or two things.

'Alex isn't here, so you're wasting your time and mine. And this house belongs to my mother. I am here, at her request, to get it ready to go on the market. And I'm asking you to leave.'

Which earned her a long, level look, an almost imperceptible softening of that slashing mouth as he told her softly, 'And I'm not going.'

Which left her floundering, almost admiring his barefaced arrogance as she sought for a way to make him. She could always phone for the police to come and evict him, and she would have done if it weren't for her uncle and Saul's position of clout at VisionWest! As it was, she was left with nothing to say except a grouchy, 'What is it you want?'

She held her breath, a band tightening around her heart as the very walls seemed to close in on them, enforcing a dreadful intimacy, the air she was trying to breathe becoming a warm, smiling sigh of wicked amusement as, long, unendurable seconds later, he said predictably, 'You know what I want. I've told you often enough.'

CHAPTER SEVEN

'How did you find this place?' The question came out on a rush. Well, she had to say something. They couldn't just stand here, staring at each other! The fraught silence, the way Saul was looking at her, as if he had just accepted delivery of a new piece of property, was shredding Fen's nerves into tiny protesting pieces.

'It wasn't difficult. Alex didn't bother to cover his tracks.' Saul patted the breast pocket of his suit jacket, his smile unnerving her all over again. 'He left phone numbers and addresses where he could be contacted during the next fortnight with Meek's secretary. I tried here first. I imagined the Edinburgh address was insurance. He can't have been too sure of you, can he? He couldn't be certain of where he'd be, and he must be fairly desperate to hear that decision.'

He walked further into the room and Fen shuddered then held herself stiffly, refusing to let him see how his presence affected her. But he didn't come too near, seemingly more interested in the few framed watercolours on the walls, bought from a struggling and not very talented artist in St Ives simply because Jean had felt sorry for him.

'I heard Jean went to Edinburgh when your affair with her husband first hit the headlines. One of the tabloids stated she'd gone back to her mother.' He still seemed far more interested in the paintings than in her, or in what he was saying. His wide shoulders looked supremely relaxed, his dark head tilted slightly to one side, as if he was trying to see more in the watercolours than was immediately obvious at a casual glance.

Fen didn't trust this sudden mood of relaxation, the soft reasonableness of his tone. And she knew she was right when he swung round on his heels, his eyes almost crippling her with their searing silver intensity as he shot out the question, 'Did he go to Jean in Edinburgh?'

She nodded, unable to look away from those glittering eyes. Her heart was hammering like a wild thing. It would be a very long time indeed before she allowed herself to get into a situation like this again. An eternity, in fact.

But never mind, she fretfully consoled herself, in a short while it would be common knowledge that the straying Alex Fairbourne was 'reunited' with his wife. So letting Saul know that her uncle was already on his way back to Jean wouldn't hurt, surely?

She wanted the whole misguided deception over and done with so that she could get on with her life without Saul Ackerman verbally branding her as some kind of high-class prostitute. She wanted to be able to tell him the whole truth, but she couldn't. Not yet. Not until that decision had been reached.

Not that the truth could make any real difference, because the wicked, almost overwhelming attraction between them wasn't going anywhere. She just hated the way he viewed her.

And something of her turmoil must have shown on her face because he, the pitiless, found pity from somewhere and he asked, with just a softening trace of compassion, 'Did he go because he wanted to, or did you push him out? It won't be easy for you to admit it if he walked out on you and left you standing. But I'd be grateful for the truth.'

Fen stared at him blankly. What possible difference could it make to him? She pushed her hands into the pockets of her dusty old jeans as the wish that she weren't looking so unkempt and grubby came out of the blue.

'The decision was mutual,' she said, sounding breathless, catching his frown of impatience when he thought she wasn't going to answer. 'We parted on friendly terms.' And that was no lie. A couple of days to help her settle in here and then he'd be off up to Edinburgh. That was what they'd planned. And she couldn't remember a time when she and her uncle hadn't been friends.

And then, catching the gleam of triumph in his eyes, she saw the trap she had lobbed herself into. She should have been quicker on the uptake and burst into tears, and wailed, and said Alex had tossed her out because he had grown tired of her, and that she would never get over it, and her heart was breaking. And would he please go away and leave her alone to grapple with her grief . . .

Instead . . .

'Then it seems you and I have a whole lot of talking to do.'

Which wasn't what she wanted to hear. Because now that he thought her 'affair' with Alex was over he would see no reason why he shouldn't take the older man's place. She should have thought of that.

Suddenly the room seemed airless, despite the breeze moving the curtains at the open windows. Fen set her teeth and walked outside, sinking down on to the wooden bench seat which, together with the picnic table, took up most of the space in the tiny front garden.

She could hear the rush of the stream as it raced its way to the sea, deep in the gorge below the narrow lane, hear the gentle, summer sound of the sea itself as it murmured on the sandy shore and lapped against the rocks. But the hypnotic sounds, the warmth of the sun as it stroked her body through the cotton shirt she wore and shimmered green and gold against the opposite hillside, failed to soothe her.

Nothing could combat the spiralling inner tension, the feeling that she was being stalked by an expert hunter; that the predator had marked out his prey; that it was only a matter of time...

So when he followed her, as she had known he would, the urge to scream at him and throw things was almost uncontrollable. But she gritted her teeth and took hold of herself and, carefully not looking at him, suggested, 'I think you should go, don't you? I can think of nothing we need to talk about.' She held herself rigid with frustration because as an exercise in self-assertion it wasn't going to cut any ice with Saul Ackerman and she hated this feeling of shameful impotence.

'Can't you?' His voice was a dark drift of warm amusement, raising the fine hairs all over her body. He arranged himself in front of her, half sitting, half leaning against the table, his long elegantly clad legs stretched out, almost touching hers.

Giving away more than she knew, Fen twisted her legs away, tucking them safely out of his reach beneath the bench, flushing to her hairline as she saw the slow white grin that told her he'd noted her knee-jerk reaction.

'Relax,' he instructed, the silver eyes all smiles now. 'We'll talk when you're ready. There's no rush.'

Her ability to relax went out of sight when he was around. But she couldn't admit to that. It would reinforce his opinion that he was in total charge; that, with the odd shove and push, he could make her do whatever he wanted her to do.

And they both knew what that was!

Forcing her eyes away from the terrifying appeal of his face, she fixed them on the horizon, the glimpse of bluey green sea that could be seen from here, glittering through the V-shaped opening between the opposing hillsides of the gorge where they ended in high granite cliffs.

'You might have all the time in the world, I haven't,' she told him stiffly. 'I'm not here on holiday, but to work.'

'Doing what? Sweeping chimneys?' The lazy curl of his voice told her he hadn't missed her filthy appearance, and he sounded as if it didn't matter, and suddenly it didn't matter to her, either, so when he tacked on, 'If you're working, maybe I could help,' she shot straight back, her mouth tugging up at the corners,

'What, in that suit?'

'That could be remedied. I could be home and back with a change of clothing in an hour.'

In that car, she didn't doubt it. But why couldn't she get it into his skull that she didn't want him anywhere near her?

'You'd be wasting your time.' She got to her feet, pretending to stifle a yawn, tapping her fingertips delicately against her perfectly even white teeth. Maybe if he thought he bored her senseless he would go away. His over-developed ego wouldn't be able to take that. 'Only I know which of my father's books and papers my mother would like to keep.'

She skirted him, trying not to look wary, more than half expecting him to put out a detaining hand. But his voice alone stopped her progress back inside the house. He didn't need to touch her at all.

'So you were telling the truth. Alex didn't set you up here. The cottage belongs to your parents?'

'My mother. I do have one, believe it or not. I didn't come down in a shower of rain.'

'I didn't imagine you did.' He pushed himself to his feet, his movements, as ever, contained and elegant. 'More like a shower of expensive perfume and starshine—despite the char-lady disguise. I thought you were lying, trying to paint the love-nest with an acceptable and homely coat of respectability.'

'I know you did.' Fen sighed. Would he always think bad things about her? A kept woman, a husband-stealer, a liar. Her soft mouth quivered but she bit down hard on her lower lip to stop it. What did it matter what he thought of her? She headed for the door, but he was there before her, barring the way.

'And she's not here? Your mother, I mean.' Narrowed eyes fastened on her mouth. The quivering started up all over again and Fen quickly dipped her head, staring at her feet because it was easier than watching the way he looked at her mouth—as if he was about to possess it with his own.

The temptation to lie, to say that yes, she was very much here, taking an afternoon nap, and would be waking at any moment, trotting down the stairs to demand an introduction, inviting him to tea and talking his head off, was very strong because it might just get rid of him.

But she knew she wouldn't lie to him, not even by omission as she had done in the past. Why deliberately set out to merit all those truly dreadful things he thought she was?

'She lives in Australia. Why the interest?'

'And your father?' He ignored her taut question, supplying another of his own. Fen gave him a bleak look. Did he never give up?

'He's dead.'

'I'm sorry.' The flare of sympathy in his eyes was the last straw. She didn't want it and wouldn't accept it. In any case, it had to be completely spurious.

'Don't be. We were never close. As far as he was concerned I was nothing more than a nuisance. Save your sympathy for my mother. She's having difficulty coming to terms with life without him!' She snapped her mouth shut, her face flooding with angry colour.

What in the name of sanity had made her sound off like that?

Her sterile relationship with her parents, particularly her father, was nobody's business but her own. She had never discussed it with anyone, not even with her uncle and aunt, because they had been there whenever Alex could spare the time from his busy schedule, watching the uncomfortable relationship at first hand, doing their best to compensate whenever they could. There had been no need actually to sit down and talk about it.

So what had possessed her? Why tell him?

'Excuse me.' Her voice was as tight as she could make it. 'You're in my way. I've got work to do. Close the gate on your way out.'

She had no very clear idea of what his reaction would be. But she certainly hadn't expected him to take her at her word. She had expected... She didn't know what. But not the sound of his car turning in the lane, the engine far too well-bred to sound in the least bit laboured as it soared away up the steep incline towards the village.

She hadn't expected him to go, to give in without a fight—no matter how laid-back and half-hearted that fight might have been. Suddenly aware that she was standing stock-still in the exact centre of the room, listening to the silence, she gave herself a mental shake and headed back upstairs.

So he had lost interest. So what? So deep joy and thank heavens—and all that stuff. She wasn't at all sure she could have trusted herself to keep him at arm's length if he had decided to put on the pressure, to subject her to his own special brand of arrogant, devilishly powerful persuasion.

He had come here, or so he had made it seem, with the express intention of talking to her. About what he hadn't said, but she would have guessed it would be more of the same—precise and, to him at least, logical reasons why she should become his mistress. But he had left without making her listen to a single thing.

Except that he had got a darn sight more out of her than she had ever intended giving.

Fen shivered, suddenly cold. She walked over to the chest of drawers and began to go through them systematically. It wasn't a task she relished, but it was the least she could do.

'We never left anything much in the way of clothes at the cottage,' her mother had said, and had added with a poignancy that had made Fen's throat close up, 'But if you come across a blue and white spotted silk cravat, send it on to me. I gave it to him for good luck. He was recording a series of talks for radio, in London. When they were done we came down to spend a weekend at the cottage with you. It was the last time we were all there together, you remember? I think he must have left it behind; it isn't among the rest of his things.'

She had made it sound as if finding that cravat was one of the most important things in the world, one more piece of memorabilia to add to the collection that kept her in close, almost physical touch with the man she had loved above all else.

Fen knew she would never love anyone with that intensity. She would never leave herself open to that kind of destruction of self.

In any case, she hadn't found it, not so far. Just odds and ends, stuff they hadn't bothered to pack and take away, tatty old gear that might come in useful on their next flying visit.

Only there hadn't been another flying visit, for any of them. Fen had been busy making her own life and her father had been doing a lecture tour in the States, her mother with him, of course.

Sorting through the drawers and dressing-table in the room they had always used when they'd been here only seemed to reinforce her growing sense of isolation, something she'd believed she had come to terms with many years ago, when she'd learned and eventually accepted that neither of her parents had ever wanted her.

So the recognition that she was hungry came as a relief, an excuse to finish up for the day, to carry the bin bag of discards down, ready to be disposed of, to decide what she would have for supper while she was having a shower, and perhaps eat outside and watch the sunset.

Dragging the unwieldy plastic bag out of the room, she started down the stairs and was halfway down, the bag bumping behind her, when he stepped into her line of vision and said, 'Let me help you.'

Fen watched in stunned silence as he took the remaining stairs two at a time, took the bin bag from her suddenly nerveless fingers and carried it down. The formal business suit had been replaced by white jeans and a black shirt, making him look too magnificently male to be true. She was too shocked by his unexpected reappearance to make a sound and when he asked, 'Where do you want me to put it?' she could only chew on her bottom lip and walk slowly down, clinging on to the banisters because her legs felt too weak to support her.

Silently, she opened the cupboard underneath the stairs and watched, wide-eyed, the play of muscles across his back as he bent to push the bulky bag into the confined space and straightened to re-close the door.

Quickly, Fen stepped back, away from him, her heart giving an unexpected, treacherous leap as she recognised the unpalatable fact that she was glad he was here. Actually glad!

Which made her a fool.

'What are you doing here?' She didn't want to be pleased to see him, to experience this shuddery awareness of him, to feel this sweet sensation of relief because he hadn't, as she had told herself, lost interest in her.

'You must have known I'd be back.' His eyes slid over her ashen face, noting the compression of the soft mouth, as if she was swallowing back the words she really wanted to say, the tension that held her tall, slender body very upright, very rigid. And he said with a softness that surprised him, 'We were going to talk, remember? But as I said, there's no real hurry. We've got all the time in the world.'

All the time in the world.

He made it sound so simple, as if they were two people getting to know each other, putting the vital physical attraction they felt for each other on hold because if the relationship were to grow and flourish it would need to put down roots, have something stronger and more meaningful to feed on than the transient desires of the flesh.

She gave him a bleak look. It wasn't like that; of course it wasn't. All he wanted from her was her body in his bed, to be used until he grew bored and moved on to someone else. And, by all accounts, he had a low boredom threshold where his women were concerned. And the talk, when it came, would be nothing more than a hundred and one reasons why he should take Alex's place.

Or what he believed to be Alex's place.

She didn't want it to be like that. She didn't want to have to listen to all those 'reasons'. And she felt nothing but a sagging relief when he said briskly, 'Why don't you go and freshen up while I put supper on the table? I brought the makings with me, courtesy of Prinny.'

Not trusting her voice, Fen shrugged and turned away, the sweet relief that flooded her making her feel giddy as she went back upstairs. She had expected him to resume his attempts to get her to move in with him. And she would never have put him down as a man who would waste time. He would decide what he wanted and go right ahead and take it. He wouldn't be interested in the waiting game.

His unpredictability worried her, but she wasn't going to waste her energies tying her brain in knots

as she tried to solve the enigma, she decided as she
stood under the shower, sluicing away the grime of
the day. She would simply be grateful for the respite,
for the relaxation of the pressure he'd exerted on every
former occasion and pretend, for as long as the strange
truce lasted, that they were two intelligent, mature
adults who were capable of enjoying each other's
company. Time enough to get back on her high horse
if and when he began to try to pressure her into his
bed again.

She rough-dried her hair and pulled on a pair of
well-worn, clean jeans, topping them with a baggy,
fine wool sweater. And didn't bother with make-up.
Why go looking for trouble?

And her lack of prinking seemed to have paid off
because the smile he gave her when she ventured back
downstairs was nice and friendly, nothing sexual about
it at all, and nothing to take exception to in the brief
appraisal of his eyes as they took in her appearance.

'Better now? Ready to eat? I've put it outside—it's
too lovely an evening to waste.'

She followed him, almost as if she had no will left
of her own. And why argue? The evening was lovely,
gold-shot with clear egg-shell blue and rich amethyst,
the chunky picnic table set with four different kinds
of cheese, a crusty granary loaf and a bottle of wine.
He had cooked a bunch of asparagus spears and they
ate it dripping with butter and Fen said, cutting herself
yet another slice of the crumbly Cheshire, 'Delicious.
I'd have put you down as a smoked salmon and cold
pheasant man, with perhaps a few quail eggs on
the side.'

She was remembering the simple picnic on the moors, too, and felt herself go warm all over as he refilled her wine glass and remarked softly, 'Perhaps life still holds a few surprises, Fen. I wouldn't have expected to find you in such isolation, cleaning out cupboards and covered in dust.' His eyes gleamed, rivalling the stars that were putting in an appearance overhead. 'Maybe the preconceptions we both started out with need rethinking.'

No 'maybe' about it! He thought she was a high-class tart, and he couldn't be more wrong. But he couldn't be blamed for that, she thought. She was beginning to feel uncomfortable now, which was a pity, because up until this moment she had been enjoying the evening and his company, marvelling in the fact that she had never felt so relaxed around him before.

But could her preconceptions about his character be way off mark, too?

Unconsciously, she shook her head. No, of course not. He was rarely seen with the same woman twice; Alex had been quite definite about that. And, even worse, his affairs had continued right through his marriage. And he hadn't turned a hair when his wife had died, which made him worse than heartless.

So she wasn't going to let herself get all relaxed and receptive. She swallowed the remains of her wine and hardened her heart. The devil was simply trying another tack, trying to get her to lower her guard. She wasn't going to forget what he wanted from her. This new, softly-softly approach wasn't going to get him anywhere. But her heart missed a beat when he told her, 'When we were on the moors you said something that made me stop and think—when I'd cooled down, anyway. You were quite right. I'd been treating you like a commodity. You deserve better than that. I'd like to apologise.'

It took her a few muddled moments to recall what she had said to him. Something about contacting her if he ever developed a heart! And that in direct response to his cutting comment that he couldn't like her because he didn't respect her, his insulting offer to pay her bills and keep her if she agreed to give Alex the push and move in with him!

So maybe he had had a rethink, decided that the crudely direct approach wouldn't work. Did he really think she was incapable of working that much out for herself? Did he think she had fluff between her ears?

'Apology accepted.' She gave him a meaningless smile and wondered why she felt betrayed. She got to her feet. 'An apology plus a delicious supper. Aren't I the lucky one! Who could possibly ask for more?' She walked the few paces to the wicket gate and held it open. 'I think we can call it quits now, don't you? Goodnight, Mr Ackerman.'

For a long, agonised moment she thought he was going to stay exactly where he was. But he did move at last, uncurling himself from the bench seat, coming towards her, his features unreadable in the growing darkness.

And when he reached for her she wished he had stayed where he was because then she could have slipped inside the house, barred the door and closed all the windows, and left him there, knowing what it was like to be outmanoeuvred for a change.

But the capacity for coherent thought left her brain as his arms dragged her roughly into the lithe hardness of his body, and the moment his mouth touched hers she was lost in the wild passion they incited in each other.

Lost. And consumed by the fiery invasion of his tongue, drawn deeper and deeper into a dark whirlpool of drugging sensation. This was what she'd once believed a kiss should be. Magic and mayhem all rolled into one, a giving and taking, a blending of two people—heart and soul—into one perfect whole.

And this was what she'd believed could never happen. After her short and monumentally disappointing relationship with Ray she had cynically disbelieved all those stories of a romantic love which somehow rapturously transported the lovers on to a plane where no one else existed, where the need to be together was paramount, as just so much wishful thinking, a lie to ensure the continuation of the species, at best, while, at worst, to subjugate the victims and make them lose their precious independence.

She had believed it to be a lie because she had believed she had loved Ray. And there had been no rapture, merely discomfort and deep embarrassment when she had lain in Ray's arms.

But now, wrapped in Saul's arms, his body pressed against hers, his hot, hungry kisses blocking her mind to everything except this wild need, she was not so sure about that. Perhaps she hadn't loved Ray at all. Maybe she simply hadn't wanted to be alone any more.

But she wasn't sure about anything, was she? How could she be, when she responded, body and soul, so completely to a man who had as good as said he despised her?

She moaned softly, in distress and confusion, and Saul's feverish, possessive mouth gentled, drawing slowly away, just a breath away. And he searched her wide and frantic eyes in the glimmer of starshine, his fingers weaving through her hair, his mouth made tender by passion as he asked her thickly, 'Did I hurt you? I'm sorry.' He leaned forward, taking her swollen lower lip between his teeth, nipping gently, his dark voice wry as he told her, 'I want you so badly. It makes me behave like an uncontrolled boy. And I can't remember when that last happened, Fen.'

'No!' She could hear the brittle thread of control in his voice and knew that the check on his desire was only just manageable. And if that thread broke, snapped by her own unbridled response to his passion, then nothing on this earth would prevent him from becoming her lover.

She wouldn't be able to stop him. She wouldn't want to stop him!

'Please go!' she pleaded wildly, snapping her head back on her slender neck, pounding his wide, rangy shoulders with her fists. 'I don't want you here—I don't!'

She was sobbing with panic. Dry sobs that tore at her throat. She couldn't believe she was acting this way, she who had always been so together, so self-

assured and calm. She was behaving hysterically and
couldn't help herself because, at some deep level of
consciousness, she knew her whole future was on the
line. Allow him to make love to her once and she
would be forever changed. Nothing would ever be the
same again.

'You don't mean that.' There was a hint of steel in
the soft dark voice as he captured her flailing fists
and held them tightly against his chest, drawing her
closer. 'You know you don't.'

She could feel the heavy beat of his heart through
the white knuckles of her clenched hands and the
temptation to unfurl her fingers within his iron-hard
clasp was enormous. She needed to lay her palms
against his chest, touch his heartbeats. But she was
fighting for her own survival and she forced out
shakily, 'I've never meant anything more. Just get
away from me. Stay away from me.'

Saul went very still. Fen raked his face with wide,
apprehensive eyes but it was too dark now to see his
expression. But she knew he would be furious. And
then he released her and her hands fell to her sides,
and his voice was perfectly calm, not one trace of
anger there at all as he told her, 'Still playing games,
I see. Let me warn you, though, such games can be
dangerous. A few moments longer and I would have
lost control and nothing would have stopped you from
becoming mine.'

Idly, he trailed a finger down the side of her face,
tracing from the fine flare of her cheekbone down to
her jaw, lingering for a tiny moment before dropping
away. It was as much as Fen could do to prevent

herself from shuddering with delicious reaction to that lingering, seductive touch.

'Maybe you like to play it rough? Is that what it is? Do you goad a man until he is out of his mind and takes you by force? Leaving you free to pretend that none of it was your fault, that you were a victim? Is that the way it was with Alex? Did the act of subduing you make him feel young and virile again? Did it make him feel responsible for you? Is that the way you get your men to pay your bills? Let me warn you again—I don't operate that way. And I don't force my women. You'll come to me because you want to, because nothing can keep you away.'

'I hate you!' She turned away, her eyes brimming with tears, but he walked past her to the gate, his voice very assured as he turned, his hand on the latch.

'No you don't. You just hate the things I make you face. And just remember—I'll be back. And I don't want you seeing Alex again. Ever. And you won't, not unless you want to ruin what's left of his career.'

CHAPTER EIGHT

FEN really didn't know what she was doing sitting
beside him in this car, being whisked away to heaven
knew where. Some place neutral, he'd said, and, like
the idiot she was now convinced she must be, she'd
once again allowed him to dictate terms.

It had been—and still was, of course—a beautiful
morning. But she'd woken feeling as if she was
smothered in dull grey rainclouds and hadn't been able
to get herself into gear and dive into the chores which
were her reason for being here at the cottage, and had
spent a couple of hours aimlessly mooching, miserably wondering what was wrong with her.

She very rarely felt depressed and was almost never
at a loose end. There was always something to do,
even if that something was merely relaxing and re-
charging her batteries. So just why she should be
feeling as if she was a thousand years old she didn't
know.

But when Saul strolled up the garden path, looking
as if he owned the place and everything in it, including her, she suddenly noticed that the sun was
shining, the sky a cloudless blue and the verges of the
narrow lane awash with wild flowers.

'Truce,' he'd said, smiling the smile she was beginning to find irresistible. 'I'm taking you to lunch.
Not my place, or yours. Neutral ground, equal terms.'

He'd parked himself on the bench seat, looking totally relaxed. 'Get ready. And don't take ages; we don't want to waste more time than we have to.'

Equal terms? He was far too confident and sure of himself. And of her. She didn't know where equality came into that kind of equation. But somehow that didn't seem to matter quite so much as it had done.

A fleeting query as to why she was giving in and letting him tell her what to do was all she had allowed herself as she'd trotted up the stairs she had trudged so heavily down a couple of hours earlier. What the heck? She hadn't been achieving anything, had she? Simply dragging herself around the place, not doing anything anyone could call remotely useful, looking and feeling like a very long, very wet weekend.

She was obviously not in the mood for clearing out the cottage. She would work better after a short break.

And she hadn't questioned the way she'd dived for the carriers she'd felt too guilty to unpack until now, tossing the garments on to the bed, her bright, glossy head tilted to one side as she considered her wickedness.

Her mouth curving, she'd selected a one-piece trousers and top in swirling psychedelic patterns in soft amber and cream with highpoints of scarlet and russet. The sleeveless bloused bodice had a cool scoopy neckline and the trouser part was softly pleated around the waist and hipline, narrowing dramatically to tight ankles.

Slipping on the highest heels she owned, she'd twisted this way and that in front of the mirror, pleased with her purchase even though she knew she should have resisted the temptation. The garment wasn't right for a pootle round the countryside but that wasn't at all important because the elegant lines, the softness of the fabric and the styling, disguised the leggy length of her and the boyishness of her figure, and that was what mattered. And wearing it made her heart lift and that was nice because it was such a contrast to the way she'd been feeling up until now.

Up until Saul had arrived, a mocking voice inside her head reminded. But Fen blithely ignored it. She was only too glad she was feeling great again and didn't much care why.

They had left the coast behind and Saul had said little apart from a few easy comments as they'd passed through a series of huddled villages, sleeping in the midday sun. And Fen had been content with that, because when they talked they usually ended up fighting, but as the car swept down into a deep tunnel of green where the hedgerow trees met in an arch overhead curiosity began to wriggle around inside her brain.

She knew, only too shatteringly well, how he could make her feel when he touched her, but that was all. She knew nothing about the man himself except what he had allowed her to see, the little her uncle had told her, and what she had learned from the few rather soulless magazine articles her uncle had kept and which Jean had given her to read when trying to persuade her to take part in the charade that had led her to the mess she was in now.

Was there anything remotely redeeming behind the mask of the ruthless predator, the mask of the man who set out to get what he wanted, who was direct to the point of insulting rudeness when he set out his needs, and his terms?

Was there a warmer, more caring and considerate character somewhere behind that mask? There was only one way to find out, and she asked, 'Did you really mean it when you said you'd see Alex's career ruined if I saw him again?'

Without realising she was doing it, Fen held her breath and silently prayed that she wouldn't be disappointed. She wanted, quite desperately, for him to deny that he could ever really be that coldly ruthless, no matter what the circumstances.

'Can it matter to you? Now?'

He sounded bored and she gave him a frowning sideways glance. So much for not wanting to be disappointed! Now that her short 'affair' with Alex Fairbourne was over she could have no further interest in the man. That was the way his mind would work. Did he lose all interest in and concern for his women as soon as the door had closed behind them after he'd kicked them out?

Of course. What else?

She shot him another dark look. They were deeper into the seemingly endless green tunnel now and the undergrowthy light made him look sinister, poles apart from the charming, charismatic character who had walked up to her this morning and declared a truce.

Heigh-ho, she thought with a deep and dreadful feeling of resignation, yet another bitter fight was obviously in the offing. And she informed him cut-

tingly, 'Of course it matters. Whatever my faults—
and according to you they're legion—I'm a loyal soul.'

She sat squarely in her seat, staring straight ahead,
and allowed him to make what he liked of that. A
ten-round verbal punch-up, she had no doubt. And
so was quite unprepared for the bleakness she heard
in his voice when he remarked, 'If you're worried
about his future, you must care a hell of a lot for
him.'

So why wasn't he plain angry? Or conceitedly
rubbing in the fact that he would make a far more
satisfactory lover than Alex Fairbourne? Much
younger, more virile, far wealthier, and free!

Fen didn't know, and she wasn't going to ask because she didn't really want yet another fight on her
hands. She had come along with him because,
strangely, there had seemed to be no choice and, even
more strangely, she had wanted to be with him. And
then they crested a hill and emerged into sunlight,
above the deep wooded valley, and everything changed
back to the way it had been before she'd asked about
Alex's career. No darkness, no undertones, merely
simple enjoyment as he told her gently, 'Arguing the
toss is pointless. Why spoil a relaxing holiday? Alex's
capabilities alone will determine his future career with
VisionWest. But as far as you're concerned, Fen, he's
ancient history.' He gave her a sideways glance that
was so uncharacteristically gentle and warm that her
toes curled in her shoes and a *frisson* of some sensation that was entirely new to her trickled its way all
down her spine. And then he added levelly, 'Forget
him; he's back with his wife, which is where he should

be. You've got to start getting your own life together, decide what's best for you. I'll gladly help, if I can.'

Help? By installing her as his mistress? A huge help that would be! If she were ever to be so foolish she would never survive the inevitable parting. She hunched her head into her shoulders, loathing the way her thoughts were leading her, telling herself that she would never behave in such a self-destructive fashion. And he couldn't make her do anything against her will. So she would waste no more time brooding about it.

She got her thoughts back in order as they passed over the brow of the hill and swooped down over a hump-backed stone bridge which crossed a shallow stream that chattered in its stony bed, and there, in the green hollow, stood a white-washed stone inn, all alone, not a village, hamlet or church tower in sight.

Fen mentally crossed her fingers. If Saul really meant what he said and her uncle's future rested on his talents, then everything would be fine. He had a lot to offer, and hopefully the big bosses would see that. For all she knew there had been no reason for him to put himself in the public eye quite so drastically.

But desperate problems called for desperate solutions, and poor Alex had been distraught over the prospect of having his programme axed. And to be on the safe side maybe she should phone him and warn him to stay well away from Cornwall—and, by implication, her—until that decision had been reached. Saul hadn't actually said he hadn't meant to carry out that threat . . .

'This is where we eat. I booked a table.' Saul eased the big vehicle into the car park and Fen squashed the thought that he must have been very sure of himself. He always was, and as she couldn't change that state of affairs she wasn't about to grumble about it. It was too nice a day and she was feeling really relaxed, despite her disquieting thoughts about the seriousness of his threat and his ominous offer to 'help' her.

They weren't the only customers, she noted. Plenty of other cars, which was probably why he had thought it necessary to book a table in advance. And although she tried not to she did flinch a little as he took her arm to lead her inside. Really, the touch of his firm, lean fingers on the bare skin of her arm was far too disturbing. It made her think things she didn't want to think. Which was why she didn't make a single protest when he calmly instructed, 'You can tell me all about yourself while we eat. I know next to nothing about you, and I intend to see that remedied.'

'There's not a lot to tell.' She sounded blithe, and she was. If telling him about herself meant she didn't have to listen to all those reasons why she should become his mistress now Alex had returned to his wife—always presuming, of course, that that rather troubled scenario still occupied his mind—then she would talk until her jaw dropped off.

He would probably die of boredom before then, though. Compared to his power, position and wealth her doings would seem totally insignificant.

But there wasn't a hint of boredom in the intelligent silver eyes as they lingered over a lunch that was fabulous enough to explain why the isolated inn was full to capacity.

'So that's why picking up languages came so naturally to you.' He smiled as he poured cream into his coffee and stirred reflectively. 'Did you mind not having settled roots?'

Fen lifted one shoulder in an elegant shrug. She had told him more about her life than she had ever told anyone. It hadn't been difficult, strange to say. Confiding in him seemed to come naturally and it was a relief not to have to watch what she said. She wasn't used to lies and deceit, all the false attitudes that had clouded their relationship—if such it could be called—from the moment their eyes had met over that restaurant table back in London.

'No, not really,' she answered truthfully. 'Maybe a little, sometimes. But travelling round the world became a way of life and I got so that even when we were settled some place—for two or three months, say—I started to get itchy feet, even though I might have made a whole lot of new friends at whatever school I was attending. I was the first to get excited when Dad had to move on. Oddly enough, my mother didn't like travelling. But her life began and ended with Dad, and she went where he went. Once she's able to come to terms with his loss I'm pretty sure she'll be more content with a proper, settled home.'

'She never wanted to make a settled home for you?' Saul put in quietly, and she shook her head, smiling easily because her parents' lack of interest in her had long since ceased to hurt.

'She never wanted me, full stop. Neither of them did. I was an encumbrance. That's not to say they failed in their duty,' she defended. 'I was adequately educated, clothed and fed.'

'But not loved,' Saul said astutely, and Fen bit her tongue because she couldn't explain about the visits from Alex and Jean and, later on, the Cornish cottage where they had spent the long summer holidays with her. Her uncle and aunt had always made time for her, taught her what a loving family life was all about.

But she couldn't tell Saul that. Not yet. But she could tell him, 'Don't feel sorry for me. I was happy. I spent four years at boarding-school here in England and then went on to get the qualifications I needed to set up as a freelance commercial translator. And during that time I only rarely saw my parents—we met up for short holidays at the cottage. So you see,' she informed him with a glint of mischief in her big amber eyes, 'I am capable of being totally independent and earning my own living. I don't need a man to keep me.'

It was as far as she dared go towards putting him right about his wrong and insulting supposition that she made a career out of being a kept woman, but she could have bitten her tongue out when she saw his eyes go bleak, caught the thread of bitterness in his voice as he beckoned the waiter over for the bill, remarking, 'So your affair with Alex was based on something deeper than his ability to pick up the tabs. I wonder if that explains your almost virginal and strenuous efforts to keep me at arm's length?'

Fen could have kicked herself as she watched the brief transaction with the credit card. Why had she reminded him of her supposedly torrid affair with Alex Fairbourne?

During the past couple of hours they had talked as they had never talked before, developing a closeness she would have believed impossible to achieve before today. And she had spoiled it with a few thoughtless words, brought all the bad things crowding in again, and knew she was going to have to suffer the aftermath when they left the inn in deep silence, the happiness suddenly drained right out of the day.

And by the time they were back at the cottage she was ready to burst into tears with tension. And telling herself that this was par for the course, that things couldn't be any different and they would always end up at each other's throats—given the type of man he was and the type of woman he thought she was, but wasn't—didn't help at all.

'I'm sorry. I've been behaving like a spoiled brat. Forgive me.'

He had pulled the car into the narrow parking space at the side of the small house and Fen stared at him, battling with a sensation that was akin to shock. Saul Ackerman actually admitting he was in the wrong? Actually apologising?

Cutting the engine, he twisted round in the driver's seat, his mouth indenting wryly as he confessed, 'I don't want to face the fact that you could have any deep feelings for Fairbourne.' He lifted a hand to touch her cheek. 'Can you understand that? I want to be the man in your life. More each day I want that.'

The touch of his fingers scorched her skin and her eyes brimmed with tears. For one crazy moment she thought she was falling in love with him. She couldn't bear it! And that melting tenderness deep in those silvery eyes was purely imagination. Of course it was. Just the effect of looking at him through a haze of stupid tears.

So she turned her head away abruptly and when he said, 'Look, let's walk ourselves into a happier mood, shall we? Come down to the beach,' she was out of the car like a shot, glad of the distraction, because if he'd said he wanted to be her man, one more time, she could well have ended up saying, Oh, yes please! instead of, Oh, get lost!

The narrow track dipped steeply down towards the shoreline, reaching the level of the rushing stream a hundred yards or so inland, and the going was difficult in the type of heels Fen had chosen to wear, but even so, when Saul scooped her up in his arms, she had to protest, 'Put me down. I don't need carrying.'

'Stop arguing, woman. At least give it a try. You might find you like it.' His arms tightened around her, giving her fair warning that he had no intention of doing as she asked, and, her body pressed so closely to his, Fen wound her arms around his neck—simply to feel more secure, of course—and gave up the fight. And maybe, just maybe, he was right. She could so easily give in entirely and let the dark tide of his passion carry her where it would.

But she wouldn't. She would find herself falling in love with him, needing him to make her complete. And that would be a very silly thing to do. She valued

her freedom and independence far too much to risk
losing it to any man, especially a man who had no
heart.

At last he released her, sitting her down on top of
one of the tumbled granite blocks that had once
formed a quayside of sorts. Long out of living memory
fishing boats had tied up here, trawling in and out of
the narrow cove to wrest a living from the sea, their
catches hauled up the steep track to the sheltered
village in rough carts pulled by wiry ponies. But other
cargoes had come this way, silently at night...

'When I was a child, I used to come down here
sometimes, when everyone else was asleep, trying to
imagine it the way it would have been when smugglers
slipped in under cover of darkness,' she confided
nostalgically.

Her eyes were smiling as she looked out over the
little bay, the sunlight dancing on the azure sea, the
golden sand, the bright rays even managing to soften
the intimidating aspect of the great granite cliffs.
Difficult to imagine muffled hoofs of burdened
ponies, the dark shapes of men as they silently un-
loaded casks of brandy and tobacco, bolts of silk...

'And did you succeed?' There was warmth in his
voice as he sat in the sun-warmed sand, his back
against the block of granite she was sitting on. He
had removed his footwear and his eyes were closed
against the glare of the sun as it bounced back off the
water and Fen's heart skipped a beat. The light picked
out the forceful lines of his spectacular features and
showed, far too clearly, the softening of the severely
sculpted lines of his mouth. But even so she recog-

nised—felt—the pulsing throb of danger that was such an intrinsic part of him.

Her throat closed up. Every time she saw him the danger escalated and the more approachable and human he seemed, the worse it got. She would do well to remember that.

'All I succeeded in doing was scaring myself half to death,' she confessed and, in spite of her determination to sound amused and at the same time impersonal, she only managed to sound breathless.

'I can imagine.' One of his hands moved lazily to remove one of her impossible shoes and then the other, and his fingers were still idly stroking a delicately arched instep as he added huskily, 'You were a lonely child. I don't like to think of you being lonely. Or afraid.'

Fen closed her eyes on a sudden pang of anguish. Did he really mean that? Did he? Or was he simply shooting a line?

And did it matter?

Frantically, she pulled her foot away from the openly erotic drift of his fingers and dropped it to the hot golden sand.

'I thought we were going to walk?' She pinned a big bright smile to her face and knew how empty it was. She was nearly crying inside.

'There's no mad hurry.' He caught up with her loping, ragged-breathed strides in no time at all. 'We have all day—and all night, too. We could stay down here and watch for your eighteenth-century smugglers. They won't frighten you if I'm holding your hand. So take it easy.' His arm went around her shoulders, comforting, warm, promising... Fen thought briefly that no, nothing would frighten her— not even a ghostly band of smugglers—if he were holding her hand. But how could she take it easy when he appeared to be doing just that? She knew him well enough now to know that when he appeared at his most relaxed he was at his most dangerous.

She must be mad to be here with him at all. She knew what he was like, what he wanted from her. So why was she here? Why wasn't she telling him to take a jump? After carefully avoiding any hint of the emotional in her casual and decidedly platonic friendships with the opposite sex ever since her farcical affair with Ray, why did every cell in her body leap with wild response every time Saul came near her?

They had reached the edge of the water, their bare feet making sharp footprints in the wet sand, and to escape the unendurable feeling of closeness engendered by the casual weight of his arm around her shoulders she bent and scooped up a pebble and with a flick of her wrist sent it skimming over the bright and glittering sea. She repeated the performance, like a mindless automaton, until he caught her round the waist with both hands, swinging her round, drawing her into his body.

His bare feet were planted wide, and the jut of his hipbones burned her up, made her heart beat too madly, her breath leave her lungs in ragged gasps.

'Fen——' His silver eyes were limpid beneath all those thick black lashes, his body told hers just how much he wanted her and she felt intolerable excitement build up inside her, feverishly expanding until it met the fierce need she felt in him, and he smiled at her, slow and sweet, sharing a secret, and his voice was thick as he told her, 'Don't keep running away. I want you in my life; you know that. But perhaps you don't know that I won't rush you, or try to make you do anything you don't want to do. We'll take things at your pace—and if that means nice and slowly, then it's fine by me.'

The hands that had dropped and were now splayed across her buttocks curved gently and pulled her more firmly into his body, his hips moving with a slow suggestiveness that threatened to blow her mind.

And it was that very threat, that very real danger, the knowledge that she was within a hair's breadth of throwing all caution to the four winds and matching his seductive movements with wilder and wantonly willing ones of her own that gave her the strength to tug herself painfully away and grate, 'One day you're going to learn that you can't always have everything you want. You've never known failure in your life, have you?'

A cold little wind whipped up out of nowhere, tossing her hair around her face. Fen brushed her fringe out of her eyes and glared at him. He looked shocked, as if he wasn't used to being told he couldn't have exactly what he wanted. It was high time he learned that lesson and, to punch her message home, she added, 'You were born knowing the world was your oyster—your father founded the hugely successful publishing company you inherited, and the profits from that helped you to buy into a failing airline and make it a legend, and the profits from that helped you grab the majority of shares in a highly competitive communications business and lash out enough cash to secure you the top position in the VisionWest consortium!' Fen shuddered with reaction, folding her arms around her tautly held body. A cloud had covered the sun but she knew that wasn't entirely responsible for the way she suddenly felt so icily cold.

'You have done your homework.' He wasn't smiling.

'It's not classified information,' she shot back. 'There have been enough articles written about you.' Lacy ripples of cold sea water were washing over her feet and she turned to head back across the beach, but his hands came down on her shoulders, swinging her round. And his eyes were bleak as he told her, 'There are other types of failure.' His voice was abrasive. 'Where human relationships are concerned I'm right down at the bottom of the class.'

Fen caught her breath and she went very still, making no attempt now to move away. That he should admit to any kind of failure was utterly new in her experience of him. His hands gripped her shoulders as if she were the rock he was clinging to as he floundered in deep, troubled waters, and she knew, with a clarity that was almost painful, that it would be fatally easy to give in to him, let him take what he wanted from her because she desperately wanted to answer the need she sensed in him, to comfort him and take away the sobering look of bleak pain she saw in his eyes.

'Do you want to talk about it?' she asked gently,
moving closer to his body warmth because the wind
from the sea was stronger now, colder. But he gave
her a puzzled glance from clouded silver eyes before
he shook his head roughly, as if to rid his mind of
his own particular devils, and then was definitely back
in control again as he answered with husky confidence,

'There's only one thing I want to discuss with you,
Fen, and that's our future relationship.' He dipped
his dark head and lightly brushed her lips with his.
'And there will be one; make no mistake about that.'

He eased her closer to his overwhelming male
strength and she went without a murmur and the way
her body turned to incandescent flame in his arms
was completely inevitable.

She gave a fluttery sigh as their breath mingled and
his mouth moved over hers with a slow, drugging sensuality that made her feel as if she was melting, melting
into him, becoming one with him.

And nothing else existed. Nothing but the quivering need deep within her as it called out to the
primitive arousal of the hard male body pressed so
closely to hers. And she was lost, abandoning her will
to his, the molten fire in her veins consuming her as
she felt the increased rapidity of his heavily beating
heart, the gasp of hunger that came from deep down
in his throat when she instinctively twined her fingers
in the thick black hair at the warm nape of his neck
and responded feverishly to his kiss.

A deep shudder rocked through him as his hands
moulded her pliant, eager body, his touch a mixture
of impatience and heart-breaking tenderness. And as

she moaned his name, her body squirming against his in a riot of blind sensation, she admitted all over again that she was lost. Her independence had been surrendered to him, and it wasn't important, not any more.

'God, how I want you, Fen!' His voice sounded ragged, starved of oxygen as he reluctantly broke the drugging kiss, cupping her flushed face with his hands, the flame of desire in his eyes meeting and holding the slumbrous passion in hers. His mouth twisted in a quirky smile, his thumbs moving roughly over her delicate cheekbones, his hard fingers twining in the bright softness of her hair. 'If you don't put an end to this I won't be able to stop myself taking you here and now.'

With the waves already swirling around their calves? A bubble of laughter broke inside her as she slowly, unconsciously, shook her head. She couldn't help him, could she? She was already lost in the type of world-shattering sensations she had never believed existed.

She knew she could break away now, walk back across the beach, and he wouldn't try to prevent her. But how could she? She hadn't the will-power. Or the desire to move out of his arms. Slowly, she ran her hands down his body, from his wide shoulders to his narrow waist, and felt him go quite still, as if he was trying to leash and control all that rampaging need.

Fen knew she was playing with fire, but she'd already been burned out of all recognition by his devastatingly hungry kisses, and, being lost, she had nothing to lose, and he gave an anguished groan and dragged her more closely into his arms, as if he would

absorb her body into his if he could, smothering her
face with the fierce passion of his mouth.

Slowly, stumblingly, they moved together, clinging
blindly to each other, inching through the water towards the sand, beyond the reach of the rapidly incoming tide. Nothing could part them now, Fen knew
that and accepted it. She was committed to him. There
was no going back. Not now.

Not until an incoming wave, much higher than the
rest, swept over them with a deluge of cold water and
left them clinging together, gasping with the shock,
and when he had his breath back Saul laughed into
her big wide eyes and told her wryly, 'You know what
they say about a bucket of cold water? Well, it's true.
But don't expect the effect to last too long.' He took
her hand and tugged her back up the beach. 'Let's go
and get dry. I'll share a hot shower and warm towel
with you, any time.'

CHAPTER NINE

FEN eyed the colourful, sodden garment on the bathroom floor without a great deal of interest. It had cost far more than she could sensibly afford and the sea water had ruined it. But she couldn't raise even a tiny flicker of annoyance over the extravagant loss.

Still shivering, she stepped under the shower and let the hot water chase the goose-bumps away.

Her body still ached for Saul and no matter how fervently she congratulated herself on her lucky escape the wanting wouldn't go away. So it was just as well he hadn't—as she had feverishly expected—insisted on sharing the shower with her but had simply asked, 'Have you a drier I could put my things in? And a towel? And you'd better get out of your wet clothes.'

An expectant and delicious shudder had snaked through her and she'd almost presented him with her back and the buttons that would need undoing, but he'd misread her reaction because he'd advised blandly, 'A shower should stop you shivering; don't hang around, just show me where to go, first.'

So she'd pointed him at the lean-to utility-room where the washing machine and drier were housed, handed him a towel and gone to take that shower. And all the time wondering if he would try to take up where they'd left off. But even though he'd said he'd share a hot shower and warm towel with her any time—and sounded as if he couldn't wait!—he hadn't made any attempt to join her.

Which meant she should be shouting, Hallelujah! giving thanks for the deluge of sea water that had dampened their ardour and saved her from her hormones.

Only the soaking in cold water hadn't dampened her ardour, she thought crossly as she stepped out at last and smothered herself with a towel. She actually still wanted him; at least, her body did, no matter how strenuously her mind dispatched all those cool and logical warnings about allowing herself to become involved with him.

Saul only wanted one thing: her body in his bed until he tired of her and moved on to the next female to take his fancy. He had been brutally honest when he'd spelled out his needs as far as she was concerned, had said not one word of love or commitment. And that wasn't good enough for her; it never could be.

But it didn't matter, surely it didn't? His lack of any genuine, lasting feeling for her was neither here nor there. She would never make love with a man unless she truly loved him. And she would never let herself fall in love because she valued her freedom and independence far too much to put herself willingly into that kind of trap.

That Saul's touch, his kisses, had demonstrated that the sexual magic she had believed to be a myth was, in truth, very real indeed only served to show her that her experience with Ray Gordon had been an unfortunate mistake. But that didn't mean she had to make another, cheapen herself by allowing all the normal feminine needs and desires she had bottled up since she'd said goodbye to Ray to lead her to indulge in a sordid affair with a man who had openly admitted he couldn't like her because he didn't respect her.

Pulling on an old pair of jeans and a soft wool shirt, she congratulated herself on sorting everything out to her own satisfaction. It wouldn't take long for his clothes to dry and when they had she would send him on his way, with a word or two of polite regret regarding her recent thoroughly wanton behaviour.

She could put all those rapacious responses of hers down to the wine she had drunk with the lunch he had given her. And hope to hell he believed her.

But the sight of the wood fire crackling in the hearth when she opened the door to the sitting-room brought a wreathing smile to her lips and she said an enthusiastic, 'Oh—how nice!' without stopping to think, looking at him without thinking, either, and then wishing she hadn't because wearing just that smallish towel wound around his narrow hips, and not another single thing, was a sexual hammer-blow of the very severest kind.

All the need, the aching, the wanting came flooding back, saturating her with the shattering desire to fly into his arms, smother that superb and almost naked body with hungry kisses and recapture the ecstasy that had recklessly whirled her into the world of the magic they had made together down on the shore.

Fen gulped, her throat feeling tight and painful as she turned away, afraid to let her eyes dwell on all that tempting masculinity for one moment longer. Her body was a traitor, and she didn't know how best to fight it. But she tried, oh, how she tried!

'Your clothes should be ready soon.' She could hear the rumbling grumble of the drier from the other room. 'Would you like a hot drink while you wait?' And now she could hear the violent drumbeat of her heart as his voice drifted over her like a cloud of lazy velvet.

'Not now. But you can feed me later.'

How late was later? Just how long did he intend to stay? Unwanted ripples of agitation skimmed over her skin. How could she tell him to go—without a hint of ferocity? How could she tell him she wasn't interested in his plans for their short-term future without betraying the fact that her wretched body had very definite and insistent ideas of its own?

'It's too comfortable here to think of moving. I'll see if my clothes are ready.'

He passed her on his way out of the room. She didn't look at him; she couldn't. Expelling her pent-up breath, Fen walked to the window and looked out. The English weather was living up to its reputation, blue skies and sunlight obliterated by thick grey cloud, rain coming in from the sea on a scudding wind. Saul was right; the little room, cosy in the light of the fire he had made, made the outdoors easy to avoid.

To insist that he left would perhaps be too extreme, she told herself, watching the rain blow inland in great grey swaths. It would be foolish to place too much vehement importance on his offer to install her as his mistress. Better—if the subject were to be broached again—to state politely but very firmly that she had no intention of becoming his mistress, now or ever. She could even smile while she said it, she told herself, trying to feel like the calm, sophisticated adult she had always believed herself to be.

And she would try to make sure he didn't touch her again. She now knew her own weaknesses where his kisses and caresses were concerned. Mind over matter, she instructed herself staunchly, bracing herself to turn and behave naturally as she heard him walk back into the room.

He was fully dressed now, thank the lord, in dry if crumpled trousers and shirt, and he said, his straight mouth quirking as if he understood her relief, and the reason for it, 'Happier now?' and then at a tangent, sinking down on to one of the comfortable arm-chairs, his endless legs stretched towards the hearth, 'Do you mind having to sell this house? Didn't you tell me it's the only remotely settled home you've ever had? And what's to happen about the furniture—are you going to have to dispose of that, too?'

'No.' Fen didn't know whether to tell him to mind his own business or not. Not, she decided, perching on the edge of a chair that was the identical twin of the one he was sprawled in. Being contentious around him didn't pay off. 'Whoever buys the cottage can have the furnishings thrown in with the purchase price, to use or dispose of as they think fit. Mother's no use for it——'

'I would imagine not—living in Australia. But you?' The softly insistent question hung on the air, demanding an answer. She didn't know why he was subjecting her to the third degree—especially over a topic as unexciting as old and rather battered furniture.

But she would answer because she would do all she could to avoid another fight, because to have that type of tension stinging through the air wouldn't be at all sensible. And against all her wary expectations he wasn't pressuring her now; it was her own treacherous body which was doing that, every centimetre of her flesh burning with the need to be in his arms again.

She was just going to have to hide that sorry state of affairs from him so she answered, hoping she sounded cool but pleasant, 'I've never had much use for material possessions. Enough clothes to fill a couple of suitcases is all I need. Anything else gets in the way and slows you down.'

'And ties you to one spot?' he inserted, watching her from hooded silver eyes, his arms crossed behind his head as he lounged back in his chair.

'Exactly,' she agreed with cool precision, but her precarious composure disintegrated, making her face burn as he enquired astutely,

'The way you were brought up turned you into a wanderer; did the lack of parental love lead to a need for emotional independence, too? Is that why you move from lover to lover—to assuage your obvious physical needs without emotional commitment?'

His question took her breath away. How dared he imply she was a promiscuous trollop? Who the hell did he think he was? All set to launch into a scathing denial, plus a blistering counter-attack because his morals were highly suspect, when all was said and done, she remembered that he had cause to believe it and felt a chill slide its way through her skin.

She couldn't tell him the truth, not yet, not until a decision had been reached about her uncle's future. And even when she did—if she did—would he believe her?

She couldn't make an answer and she couldn't simply sit here, his mesmeric eyes probing right into her soul. So she said, sounding wooden, 'You wanted me to feed you. Excuse me...' And she pushed herself out of the chair and into the kitchen, asking herself what she thought she was doing, offering to give him supper when all she'd wanted was for him to go and leave her in peace, give her the space she needed to get over this monumental physical attraction.

It had been a knee-jerk reaction, she mourned. Desperate to get away from him and his probing insulting questions, she had grasped at the excuse of preparing a meal without thinking it out.

And her tactical retreat hadn't achieved a thing because he was right behind her, big and dark and much too masculine, his voice dry as he remarked, 'A subject you don't want to pursue, I take it. Not to worry; I'll root out your motivations some other time. What are we eating?'

His words, if she had any say in it! she thought bitterly. His close proximity in the small kitchen, the mess she was in—a mess of her own and her uncle's making—made her want to relieve the stress she was under by lashing out. At him. But she controlled the dangerous urge and said ungraciously, 'Omelette. And only by helping do you get to stay in the kitchen.' She dived in the fridge and came out with a bag of mushrooms. 'You can peel and chop these.'

'Whatever you say, little cat. Things might be different later. In fact I can guarantee they will. But for now, at least, you're the boss.'

His eyes were laughing at her and her breath clogged in her throat. She felt punch-drunk whenever he looked at her and she wished she'd been determined enough to give him a glass of wine and send him back to sit by the fire, out of her way. Because the hands that were now busily preparing the mushrooms were beautiful, strong, deft and sensual. And try as she would she couldn't stop thinking of the way they had made her feel as they'd stroked her body into mindless capitulation.

And what had he meant when he'd said things would be different later? She wouldn't give herself three guesses because she already knew the answer, and quite how she was going to be able to fight both him and her own instinctive response to him she didn't know. But she'd come up with something. Somehow.

Edgy, and showing it, she thought self-disgustedly as the plates she was sliding into the warming oven rattled together like castanets. And Saul would know it, too. She sometimes felt he knew exactly what she was thinking, how she was feeling, as if there were a bond between them. Which was nonsense.

Not looking at him because she couldn't bear to see the speculative smile in his eyes, she got on with what she was doing, her growing uneasiness responsible for the song and dance she was making of the simple chores. And it was Saul who actually eased the

tension that was gripping her by the throat, es-
chewing the formality of eating at the table, finding
trays, the modest stock of wine Alex had insisted on
bringing here for her, selecting a Valdepeñas and ush-
ering her through to the sitting-room where they ate
from the trays on their knees in front of the fire.

And it was Saul who removed the plates they had
finished with, poured her more wine, revitalised the
fire with an armful of dry logs and drew the curtains
against the darkness and rain.

Strangely enough, she felt secure with him, like this.
Just the two of them and a strand of unforced conversation that ranged over topics that were as diverse
as they were interesting. And with his own brand of
devilish ease he had seduced her into total relaxation,
so that not even one alarm bell sounded when he asked
smoothly, 'What will you do and where will you go
after you've finished here?'

Fen shrugged dismissively, her tawny eyes like gold
jewels in the firelight, lazy and warm. She twisted the
stem of her wine glass slowly between her long, slender
fingers and told him, 'Look for a way to earn my next
crust and, when I've found it, go to wherever it is.'

She was too contented to be bothered to tell him
that her next scheduled job didn't start until later in
the summer, in Italy, or that, due to her own extrava-
gance, she would probably have to find something to
fill the gap. And she was totally unprepared for the
harsh rasp of his voice as he admitted, almost reluctantly, as if the words had been torn from him against
his will, 'I worry about you. Don't ask me why, Fen,
but I do.'

It was then that the treacherous feeling of relaxation he had so cleverly induced flew right out of the window, and her heart was thudding like a steam-hammer as he said through his teeth, 'Why run round the world like a gypsy when I can offer you a roof over your head and a bed to sleep in? You know the way we are together—one look, one touch and we both go up in flame.' He went to straddle the hearth, his eyes dark and frowning, his mouth a straight line, and cut off her automatic protest with an impatient slash of his hand. 'Don't even think of trying to deny it. I hate it when women lie. Together, you and I could make magic, Fen. And you know it.' His mouth twisted in a smile that held no warmth, no humour. 'This may not be the most romantic offer you've ever had—I don't believe in dressing basics up with pretty words to make them seem more palatable—but I need someone permanent in my life. Not just anyone with a beautiful face and endless legs. I need you. And I think you need me.'

Could he hear the thunder of her heart in the sudden silence of the room? The things he said made her want to cry. She gripped her wine glass until her knuckles went white and he took it from her, putting it down on the hearth, his movements taut, as if he was under some kind of strain.

Fen closed her eyes as anguish surged through her. Need him? How could she possibly need him?

If she agreed to what he was suggesting she would be pushing the self-destruct button with a vengeance. So now was the time to haul herself together, finally to get things straight, let him know that in no circumstances whatsoever would she agree to become his live-in lady. And she looked at him then, held the intensity of his narrowed eyes and forced a vinegary note into her voice as she derided, 'Why should I need you? What could you possibly offer that I couldn't get from any one of a hundred other men in a hundred other places?' and watched his face go tight with rage.

But he was good at controlling it, she had to give him that, because his tone was perfectly level as he came back, surprising her all over again, 'I said I wanted to help you, and I meant it. You need someone to take you in hand, and I could do it. I understand why you are the way you are. You must have loved your parents when you were a young child, and you would have felt deeply hurt and insecure when you discovered you weren't wanted.'

Even before he moved she knew he was going to touch her and she did nothing to stop him when he took her hands in his and drew her to her feet. How could she stop him when every fluttery beat of her heart was telling her how much she wanted to be near him, to feel his hard body burning against hers, to know again the way his mouth felt against hers?

But the touch of his hands around her small waist was loose, almost careless—as if he knew she had lost all will to fight him, that he held her, now and always, with the simple power of his presence; knew, with that wicked insight of his, that his being near her was enough to subdue the waywardness in her. He was masterful, he was magic, he was spawn of the devil...

He held the dreaming, desire-hazed gold of her gaze with the silver intensity of his eyes and the tone of his voice alone told her of his heightened need as it deepened to a husky caress.

'Without knowing that they did it, your parents taught you to back off from any emotional commitment. I could teach you to give that commitment, help you to learn that giving doesn't mean losing, that giving can only help you to grow as a human being.'

Seductive words to match the light, seductive touch of his beautiful hands. She felt as if she was drowning in warm honey. So sweet, so soft, so tempting...

Biting down hard on her lower lip to remind herself that the devil was well-versed in saying the things that poor misguided mortals wanted to hear, Fen queried, just to set the record straight, because he couldn't care for her, not the essential her within what he saw as the nubile outer packaging, 'You said you wanted me in your life. So how permanent is permanent?' And, without knowing she did it, she held her breath. And expelled it on a pang of pain as he told her what she now knew she hadn't wanted to hear.

'Nothing lasts. I've learned that the hard way. I suppose I mean for as long as we both want to stay together. We would be good together, good for each other, and you could learn what it's like to put down a few roots. You've already seen my home. It's a happy house, Fen. You would be content there.'

There. With him. Oh, she could be happy, blissfully so if things were different. If he loved her, if he wanted her for always...

As soon as she'd walked into his home she'd had the strangest feeling that the place welcomed her, that there, if anywhere, she could put down roots. But there would be bitterness, too. And fear. Both clouding whatever joy was on offer because sooner or later he would tire of her and ask her to go. She would never put herself through that type of hell.

'You want me to replace all those one-nighters.' Her mouth went hard as she fought the overwhelming need to agree to anything he said, everything he said. 'Feeling your age, Saul? Is the chase getting too much for you and losing its thrill?' She tried to pull away; whatever distance she managed to put between them would be welcome—far more than welcome, it was vitally necessary—but he refused to let her escape, his hands tightening around her body, making her go rigid with distress.

'I don't go in for one-night stands, if that's what you're implying. I never have. Sanchia was the expert in that field.'

The bitterness in his voice caught her unawares, reluctant curiosity easing the rigidity from her body as she asked, 'Who is Sanchia?'

All the tension that had drained from her seemed to have entered into him because the big body so close to hers was taut with it now, his voice hard and clipped as he answered shortly, 'My wife, past tense. She died.'

The wife whose death had, by all accounts, left him totally unaffected. Alex had said something about that short-lived and troubled marriage—that there had always been someone else in it, muddying the waters. She had automatically assumed that Saul and his womanising had been responsible for the breakdown.

Had she been wrong?

This tension, this bitterness, seemed to suggest that she had and she searched his closed features for some further clue but he turned away, his hands releasing her. And, far from feeling grateful for the respite she had so recently craved, she deeply regretted the chilling distance that he had put between them and said quickly, with instinctive sympathy, 'Do you want to tell me about it?'

The ruthlessly handsome face was hard as he faced her again, the black brows frowning. Then he shook his head, as if he had reached a decision, and took the two paces back to her again, his brow clearing as he told her, 'Do you know, Fen, I think I do?' He took her hand, his lean fingers twining with hers. 'My marriage isn't something I discuss. Ever.' His tone was dry. 'But I've got the feeling I can break that rule for you.'

He sank down into the armchair and would have taken her with him but she wasn't stupid enough to let herself get that close and compromised by dropping to the hearthrug by his feet. Her palms were damp with sweat, her pulses racing. Was he breaking his own rules because he thought she was in some way special to him, worthy of his confidences? Or was this to be another of his master-strokes?

One of his hands was resting on her shoulder, the strong fingers burning through the fine wool of her shirt. Fen stared into the fire, at the yellow flames licking around the logs, her mind in turmoil. She ought not to crave his confidences—they would only burden her further with this fateful feeling of closeness, the closeness that seemed to grow with sneaky inevitability each time they encountered one another.

She should never have invited him to talk about his marriage. She should have told him it was getting late and asked him to go. Would she ever learn sense where he was concerned?

No. She answered her own question with a delicate shudder as his hand gently stroked the nape of her neck. No. Never. To her own deep shame she was as weak as water when his terrifying sexual magic came into play. She leaned back against his knees, despising herself yet incapable of acting any other way, and heard the abrasive note in his voice as he told her, 'I'd never considered marriage as a viable option before I met Sanchia. I was an achiever, and proud of it, and I couldn't foresee the day when a woman could take even a small part of my mind away from my business career. Being married, I always knew, would mean that there would inevitably be circumstances when my wife would have to take first place. So I played the field—never anything serious and no hearts broken.'

'But that changed when you met your wife,' Fen put in dully, hating the feeling of being hurt. Why should his admission that he had once loved a woman so deeply that he had willingly relegated his meteoric career to second place cut her like a sharp-pointed blade? All she should sensibly feel was a mild surprise that the hard man was capable of any kind of tender emotion.

'No, not at first. It wasn't a case of love at first sight. Far from it.'

She heard him drag in a sigh. His fingers were playing with the lobe of her ear, but absently, his mind obviously far away. Fen ground her teeth and stared blindly into the fire. His mind might not be on what he was doing, but hers was!

The soft and tormentingly erotic—even if mindless—pressure of those sensual fingers was responsible for the rising tide of fever through her blood. And if there had been any strength left in her limbs at all she would have scrambled to her feet and walked away, away from all that danger, but her rioting feelings went unnoticed by him because his voice was dull, showing no emotion whatsoever as he went on, 'I met her at a party. She was South African, paying a visit to the old country to stay with an aunt and some cousins in London. I barely noticed her. Then we started to run across each other socially quite regularly, and I began to pay more attention. She wasn't beautiful—she was barely even pretty. A little too short, a little too plump, her blonde hair too fluffy. Nothing like the women I'd dated up until then. She would never turn heads but she made me think of home-cooked Sunday lunch, gardens and apple pie and babies in nurseries.' He shifted his knees apart, his hands going to her shoulders to settle her between them, his fingers resting lightly on her collarbone. 'And it suddenly occurred to me that I was missing out. I'd amassed a fortune but wasn't using it. All at once I wanted to hunt for a house I could make into a home, have children to inherit what I had made. Quite suddenly marriage seemed sensible. And when

I made my wedding vows I meant them because, in spite of what you may think, I do have some integrity.'

But he hadn't said he'd loved his wife, Fen thought on a note of ignoble exultation as she trawled backwards and forwards through his words. Then she flattened the feeling because she knew it shouldn't matter. Mustn't matter. And she asked, sympathetically, she hoped, 'So what went wrong?'

'What always goes wrong with dreams? You wake up eventually,' he said, the bitterness back in his voice, self-derision, too, and that showed her how badly he'd been hurt, and she dragged her lower lip between her teeth, thankful he couldn't see her face. 'I married the illusion and had to try to live with the reality. There was nothing sweet and wholesome and domesticated about my wife. She was rotten with disease and the disease was sex. Any man, any time, anywhere. I tried to get her to seek qualified help, tried to make the marriage work and although she was always suitably contrite when her indiscretions were discovered it would never be very long before she got involved with another man. She didn't know the meaning of love, only lust. I was never enough for her and I later discovered, after her death in a road accident, that her parents had shipped her back to England because the scandals she was creating back home were becoming impossible for them to live with.'

'I'm sorry.' Fen couldn't think of anything else to say. And what use was 'sorry'?

'Don't be.' He was leaning forward now, his head dipping so that his dark hair mingled with the gold of hers. 'I lived through it and came to terms with it.

Kept it all private, as far as I could—but I'm glad I told you. I was married, and it was a total failure. I wanted you to know. Now...' He drifted into a silence that was thick with things unspoken and Fen tried to find all the iron resolve that seemed to run away and hide whenever he was close.

But the pads of his fingers were stroking the upper curves of her breasts, branding her through the soft fabric of her shirt, and her pulses raced out of control and a great sob built up in her lungs because she now knew the reason behind his bleak statement touching on his failure in human relationships.

He'd been talking about his marriage, blaming himself for the breakdown when it hadn't been his fault. Just as she had leapt to all the wrong conclusions and heaped all the guilt on to his wide shoulders.

'Shall we just forget about it?' he was saying, the fingers of one hand busy now with her shirt buttons, and she found the strength of will from somewhere to drag herself to her feet and say with breathless haste, the words tripping over each other,

'That's the most sensible idea I've heard in a long time! And the second is a nice hot cup of coffee. Stay right where you are. I'll get it.' And she rushed into the kitchen as if the devil himself were on her heels.

And he was, she thought as she subsided weakly against the work surface. Oh, he was! Insinuating himself right into her heart.

'Oh, knicker elastic!' she growled under her breath as she made a shaky attempt to fill the kettle. How could she have let this happen? In spite of her long-held determination never to fall in love, be cheated of her freedom and independence, he had trapped her. She had fallen in love with Saul Ackerman and she would never be her own woman again. The prospect didn't bear thinking about!

CHAPTER TEN

SHE would get over it, of course she would, Fen assured herself with more fire than conviction as she made the coffee. She would have to, if her chosen way of life were to make any sense, be at all tolerable.

All she had to do was act her heart out, not let him even get a hint of what she really felt. If he even guessed she had fallen in love with him he would move in on her with all the deadly charisma at his command and she knew she would never be strong-minded enough to fight him.

Frowning at her still-shaky hands, she loaded a tray, squared her shoulders and dragged in a very deep breath.

She would be bright and breezy, letting him know she was quite definitely her own woman, and proud of it. But not unsympathetic, of course, because by taking her into his confidence, when he had never mentioned the true misery of his marriage to another living soul, he had bestowed on her a very special kind of honour.

But she would remind him of all his own affairs, following on the death of his wife, and, in doing so, remind herself, ram the facts firmly into a brain that seemed to have gone temporarily on the blink.

And she would definitely keep distance between them, even if it meant drinking her coffee while she walked backwards round the room. It would be fatal if he touched her.

Swallowing the lump of utter desolation brought on by the crippling knowledge that she would never again know the bliss of his kisses and caresses, must send him away and never see him again, she carried the tray through to the sitting-room, gave him a cup and handed him the cream. Then she took her own cup to the far side of the room and sat on one of the straight-backed chairs that stood beside the gate-legged table under the window.

'Don't try to look prim, Fen. It doesn't suit you.'

He was regarding her with something that looked suspiciously like amusement. And tenderness? Whatever—it curled her toes. She looked quickly down at the cup in her hands and the sexy, warm drift of his voice enclosed her, and a sweet stab of desire shafted deep inside her; his voice alone could beguile her, and almost did as he commanded softly. 'Come here. Come to me.'

The temptation to obey was wickedly strong, and had to be resisted. She knew only too well what would happen if she went anywhere near him. He wanted her and she loved him and the equation was danger-ously explosive.

Putting her cup down on the table at her side be-cause the trembling of her hands was a certain give-away, she gazed at a point beyond his head and told him with a lack of heat that did her credit, 'I won't be your mistress. So do us both a favour and don't mention it again.'

'No?'

He didn't sound disturbed by her statement and her eyes were clouded with suspicion as she flicked a look at him through her lashes. A hint of a smile played round his slashing mouth and she could have drowned in the look in his eyes.

'No!' She shook her head then dragged herself together. She was beginning to get too vehement and that wasn't the way she had planned to play this scene. She had to stay cool and in command of the situation. If she lost her temper then things could get out of hand. 'I know what you think of my morals, but I don't hop in and out of men's beds as if I've got springs under my feet, believe me. And by all accounts the women in your life don't hold your interest for longer than yesterday's newspapers. I mean,' she tacked on hastily in case he thought she hadn't believed a word he'd said about the reason for the breakdown of his marriage, 'the women you've had since your wife died.'

'Ah.' He shook his head slowly, his eyes glinting. 'All three hundred and sixty-five of them—one for each day of the year.'

Fen swallowed painfully. She wasn't getting the message through. He wasn't taking her seriously. He had talked glibly about her being a permanent part of his life and had gone on to admit that meant only for as long as they wanted to stay together. Which, in turn, meant until he grew tired of her. He wouldn't put up with a mistress who was beginning to bore him.

And she didn't want to be his mistress, always wondering if today was the day he would tell her the time had come to split. She wanted . . . she wanted . . . what

she could never have, and she would do well to remember that and act accordingly, she growled at
herself. And told him more tartly than she had ever
intended, 'I won't be one of a long, long line. I'm
sure you meant your offer to flatter, but I'm going
to have to decline.' Even though being with him, close
to him in every possible way, was the one thing her
poor silly heart craved above all else.

His face was tense as he got to his feet and walked
towards her with slow deliberation. And his voice was
biting as he threw out, 'Sanchia died four years ago.
And the last woman I took to my bed left it after an
affair that lasted for a little under a week. That was
more than two years ago. I have a normal man's needs
but I found that I took little joy in such cold coup-
lings. You won't be one of a line—long or short. You
are, and will be, unique. Satisfied?'

He was standing right over her, naked anger in his
face. She had obviously touched him on a very raw
spot indeed, but she shook her head speechlessly yet
very emphatically, the wetness of tears on her lashes.
Only his love, a lifetime's commitment, could satisfy
her. And that she was not about to get.

And then the anger sluiced from his face, leaving
it grey and drawn. And he said in a voice she scarcely
recognised, 'Am I really so unlovable, Fen?'

And during the fraction of time it took her to rake
his anguished features with the pained compassion of
her eyes she knew what he meant.

He had not meant love in the literal sense. Rather,
she knew, he was referring to the failure of his marriage, the failure of the relationship he'd entered into

with the woman he'd spoken of, over two years ago now, the way he'd corrected her when she'd said he'd never known failure in his life.

And right now he believed that he had failed again, with her, that he could never sustain a close human relationship. And, loving him, she couldn't bear it. And she was on her feet and in his arms before she had time to think, his totally unexpected display of vulnerability making her ache to comfort him.

'You mustn't think that. Not ever!' Her hands looping behind his head, she covered the side of his face with tiny, feather-light kisses, not a single thought of self-preservation in her mind, only thoughts of him, of what he was feeling. His skin felt grainy beneath her lips, and it tasted slightly of salt, and of something that was indefinably masculine.

Fen heard the rough sound as his breath caught in his throat, and then his arms pulled her close and his mouth covered hers in feverish possession. She whimpered, not from panic but from sheer blinding pleasure, and he knew that, because his mouth gentled, the pressure lighter but even more erotic as his tongue parted her lips, making her drown in a whirlpool of dark delight as she clung with wild abandon to the strong, predatory passion of his hard male body, exulting in the thrusting evidence of his arousal, the crazed tumult that sang through her blood as he crooned hoarsely against her lips, 'Oh, yes, oh yes, Fen!' then slipped his hands beneath the hem of her shirt, finding her small yet pertly firm breasts and holding them in the palms of his hands, caressing the silky soft flesh until she arched her spine, mewing softly in her throat until he disposed of her shirt with lean, impatient fingers and gave her the wild pleasure she had unconsciously been begging for, suckling each taut nipple in turn, guiding the erect, rosy buds to the moist wickedness of his mouth with gentle, insistent, stroking fingers.

Her own eager fingers threaded in the soft springy darkness of his hair, Fen moaned with the pleasure that was almost a pain and knew there would be no going back. Not for her. Not ever. Her principles, the self-preserving need to protect herself from emotional damage, slipped out of sight. Because she loved him as she had never believed it would be possible to love any man, and this was right. It was good. So good...

And while his mouth paid homage to her breasts the fingers of one hand dealt with the button at the waistband of her jeans, easing them down over her hips, his hands following, stroking the satin flare of her hips, the slender lines of her thighs until she thought her heart would burst with wanting him, needing him, loving him.

'You are so beautiful, Fen,' he said softly. 'You are perfection, a hymn of delight. Every inch a poem.' His eyes devoured her unashamed nakedness, as if storing away the image for all time. And he was all possessive, demanding male as he growled throatily, 'And you're mine. All mine.'

He swept her into his arms, and she went willingly, with tumultuous exultation in her heart, her blood singing as he carried her upstairs and placed her with almost reverent care on the bed, looking down at her, his eyes black with passion as he removed his own clothing and joined her, gathering her to the aroused and savage masculinity of his body, covering her face with kisses, his voice low but triumphant as he whispered, 'From the moment I first saw you I knew we were meant for each other. And I knew you'd be mine—willingly, wantonly, wickedly...'

And then there were no more words, no need for them when hands and lips said all there was to say, when body worshipped body and flesh adored flesh, when he showed her the meaning of ecstasy beyond description and her fevered, loving body answered his with glorious, unstinting generosity.

Fen woke as the sunlight shafted in through the uncurtained window and touched her face, her lids lifting dreamily. She felt radiant with love and had lost count of the number of times they had made love to each other during the long, glorious night.

What price her freedom and independence now? she thought dazedly as she gently extricated herself from a possessively outflung arm. She belonged to him, now and for all time, enslaved by a depth of passion and love that was impossible to deny.

He was sprawled out on the bed, the deep, slow rhythm of his breathing barely disturbing the olive-toned magnificence of his broad chest. Unable to resist, she traced the outline of flat male nipples with the tip of her finger, felt him stir and made herself stop what she was doing. If he woke now they would make love again, and there was a lot she had to say to him before that happened. So much to clear up, so much to straighten out before they could move forward into their future.

Momentarily, her golden eyes clouded. How much future would he allow them to share together? Until they no longer wanted to stay together. The answer was cold, solid fact, but facts could be altered, given a different perspective, couldn't they?

It would be up to her to make damn sure that he wanted to stay with her always, she vowed with soaring optimism.

Gingerly, she wriggled off the bed and crept out of the room, gathering fresh clothes as she went. She would love him always, stay with him always, go where he went. The only freedom she needed now was the freedom to express her love. And if she were ever to bear his children she would never allow her love for him to freeze them out. Between them, she and Saul would give them the security of knowing they were loved and wanted, that having them cemented and strengthened their own love, making it grow, ensuring that there was enough to spill over and encompass them, too.

Fen pulled her dreaming thoughts up short. There would be no children without marriage and she was definitely leaping too far ahead, allowing the blissful aftermath of a night of passionate, glorious love to blind her to reality.

He had never mentioned the word marriage in connection with her. And why should he? He believed she changed lovers as regularly as other women changed library books. But he might change his mind, the treacherous voice of optimism put in, when he learned the truth about her relationship with Alex.

Hugging the hope to her, she hustled under the shower, not taking time to dry herself properly, so that the light T-shirt and skimpy shorts she dragged on clung revealingly to her woman's body.

She felt more alive, more feminine, more meltingly soft than she had ever felt before. Ecstatically happy, too, the only slight niggle in her mind the question of whether he would want to commit himself permanently to her when he learned that, apart from Ray—who had come nowhere near awaking her true potential as a woman—she had had no other lover.

But even that question mark couldn't quell the bubble of sheer joy that ran through her veins like champagne. And the sky was a brilliant blue again, the early morning sun already warm, and through the door she had flung open she could hear the surf pounding against the shore as last night's storm still swelled the ocean.

Utter perfection! And she was humming under her breath as she took breakfast things out to the picnic table and when Saul padded up behind her and wrapped his arms around her waist, pulling her back into his body and nuzzling his lips to the side of her neck, her heart trembled with excitement.

'I'd intended to bring you breakfast in bed. And lunch. And supper.'

She felt the warmth of his breath, the warmth of his smile against her exultantly sensitised skin and when she twisted round in his arms she felt the potency of his arousal and almost lost her resolve.

But she clung to it, even when the slow, suggestive movements of his hips threatened to drag it from her and fling it to the four winds.

'I've got something I want to talk to you about.' If she sounded breathless she had the perfect excuse. The sweetly tender sensation in her loins was sent soaring to full, demanding life by the things he was doing to her, making her feel.

He smiled, his sinful silver eyes gleaming as he put a slowly lingering kiss on her swollen mouth. 'You certainly do have something, but I can think of better things to do with it than talk about it.'

'No—be serious!' She was flushed, her mouth trembling on the brink of laughter, her body trembling on the brink of something else entirely, and he silenced her protest with a series of tiny linked kisses, assuring her huskily.

'Oh, I am, I am. I've never been more serious. Come back to bed. Let's celebrate the start of a relationship that's going to be fantastic for both of us.'

'I mean it.' Her voice was hoarse as she twisted out of his arms, her loins throbbing in time with the hectic beat of her blood. 'There's something I need to say to you first.'

'I take heart from that "first"!' He grinned at her, his hands on his hips. He looked totally magnificent despite the rumpled clothes, his tousled black hair and shadowed growth of beard making him look dangerously piratical. 'Go right ahead.'

'Over breakfast.' She could be firm when she had to be, she congratulated herself giddily, hurrying back into the kitchen, her heart nearly tripping over itself.

And back with the steaming filter jug, a rack of fresh toast, she edged round the table, choosing to sit opposite him, her eyes checking that everything was present.

Orange juice, butter in a brown earthenware pot, honey. Did he like honey? There were so many things she didn't know about him, and each new discovery would be a joy. As her eyes met his across the table she was swamped with her love for him, too swamped to get a word out as she shakily poured coffee and chilled juice for them both and watched him spread butter on hot toast, the devilishly clever, lean fingers moving with uncalculated precision.

Cutting his toast into four equal quarters, one dark brow drifted upwards. 'Well? What's so important, sweetheart?'

The easy endearment took her breath away, implied something far gentler, more loving than lust. Fen grappled for words and told him, her love for him making her voice ragged, 'Alex Fairbourne is my uncle, my mother's brother. Our ''affair'' simply didn't exist, needless to say. The only substance it had was in the minds of those people who chose to believe the salacious innuendos coming from the Press.'

Up until this morning she had been determined to keep the truth from him until her uncle's future with VisionWest had been decided. But falling in love with Saul, giving herself to him, accepting him as her lover, had changed all that. The most important thing now was for him to know the truth about her. He wouldn't punish Alex for the deception; he was too strong a character to indulge in that kind of spite. And, even if he didn't love her, he wanted her desperately, felt some tenderness for her, and she was sure he would do nothing to hurt her uncle and, through him, her.

She was watching him closely and he had gone very still. His unforgettable features were quite without expression. His breakfast abandoned, he regarded her from dark, sombre eyes.

'And? There has to be more than that.'

There was, and she told him, her voice going thinner as she realised that something was going drastically wrong. Told him that, far from being a career-mistress, she had only had one lover before him, and that fiasco had happened a long time ago. Told him of her uncle's very real fears that falling viewing figures meant the inevitable axing of his show; of Jean's hare-brained idea to get him back in the public eye, present him as the sexy heart-throb who had once had women swooning in the aisles—and could do again if the female viewers could somehow be persuaded to see him as a mature and macho male who could still attract a much younger woman.

'It was a silly idea,' Fen conceded weakly, wishing he would say something, inject some comment of his own instead of looking at her with those cold, dark eyes. Even the warm sunlight failed to soften the harsh austerity of his hard, slashing features. 'And once the story got out we simply went along with it——'

'Laughing behind your slender white hand.' He left the table, his movements perfectly controlled. His eyes met hers with the impact of an electric shock. 'No one makes a fool of me, not even a woman. Especially not a woman. Never again.'

He was talking about Sanchia, the way she'd acted during their marriage. Fen could excuse his bitterness. But she, Fen, had never set out to make a fool of him. Circumstances had overtaken them and had made a confession, until now, out of the question. She had to try to make him understand that. If it was the last thing she did, she had to do that.

But he was leaving, striding down the path as if he couldn't get away from her quickly enough, and she followed just as soon as her stunned and bewildered brain allowed her to jump to her feet.

'Saul!' He was already unlocking the door of his car and her mouth went dry with fear. This couldn't be happening, it couldn't. How could he walk away from her, after last night? How could he do this to her?

Her huge eyes pleading, she wrestled with the wicket gate, her movements clumsy and uncoordinated in her panic. He didn't even look at her, and her anguished, 'I love you, Saul——' was drowned in the hungry growl of the engine as he backed the car up the steep incline of the track, sending pebbles flying, scattering stones beneath the wheels.

In the grey-green shadow of the rock Fen dabbled her toes in the soft salt water of the pool, watching the glimmer and glitter, the refractions of gold and silver light on the broken surface. She dragged in a long breath of sparkling air and tried to relax.

Tomorrow she would be leaving this lovely and secluded place forever and she would never come back. Jean and Alex had arranged to collect her and the things her mother would want sent on to Australia, and that would be that. She would be saying goodbye to a chunk of her past. And finally, irrevocably, to Saul.

It had been a week, almost to the hour, since he had walked out on her, too bitterly angry to listen to another word from her. And he'd left her dying inside, rigid with shock. It had been quite some time before she'd felt able to pull herself together and then, by some miracle, she had found the energy of twenty, tackling the remainder of the chores like a tornado, rarely stopping to eat and only falling into bed when exhaustion forced her to.

She hadn't cried, and that hadn't surprised her. She was too empty and drained to find tears. All the emotions he had forced into wildly erupting life seemed to have atrophied.

But who needed emotions, anyway? They only made people make a mess of their lives. She could live without them. She would darn well make sure she lived without them!

Wading through the rock-pool, her bare feet found firm, warm sand and she headed for the line of breaking surf, sunlight falling on her bright hair, caressing the bare skin of her long, long legs beneath the tiny cotton shorts, burning through the shabby, oversize T-shirt that came down to her thighs.

The only crumb of comfort she could pick out of the sorry tangle of her situation was the fact that, contrary to the dreadful fears she'd had when she'd emerged from the shock of Saul's reaction to her confession, Alex hadn't been booted out of VisionWest.

Twenty-four hours after Saul had stormed out Jean had phoned from Edinburgh, barely sounding sane.

'Alex can't talk to you—to anyone! He's too hyped up, bless him! Just think—a weekly chat show—not a series—weekly! They're offering him a long contract. Laurence Meek phoned half an hour ago. They've been viewing tapes of his shows, apparently. Laurence said he was a natural interviewer—remember he always did a short celebrity interview slot on *Evening With Alex*? They've decided he's to host his own chat show; we're beside ourselves with excitement . . .'

At least she could be thankful that Saul hadn't taken his bitter anger out on Alex; she would never have forgiven herself if he had. So there were no loose ends to tie up now, and there would be few regrets. Saul had worked his wizardry and compelled her to fall in love with him. And, in doing so, had underlined her former and definitely saner opinion that it was safer and less complicated to travel through life alone. Footloose and heart-whole.

And she would be that again, she assured herself tightly as she flung a pebble far out into the surging waves. She would put Saul Ackerman out of her mind just as soon as she started out on the rest of her life.

And the rest of her life began tomorrow.

And as for today, she would simply relax and soak up the sun, try to unwind and decide what to do with the next few weeks. She could always stay on at the cottage—being on hand, she could show any prospective buyers around—but she couldn't afford the luxury of such idleness and she couldn't afford the pain. Everything reminded her of Saul, of the way he had touched her, made love to her, the things he had said, the silver gleam of his eyes, the eloquent beauty of his strong, lean hands... And the pain was fierce. So staying on here was not the way to cut him out of her mind.

Jean and Alex had said she could stay with them until it was time to take up her next scheduled job in Italy. But she was too independent to accept charity, even from people she loved, and their other, almost grudgingly offered suggestion seemed the best she could hope for at the moment. Two of their friends owned a small hotel near Truro and were desperately short-staffed; they needed someone who was willing to turn a hand to anything in return for bed and board and a small pay packet.

They had made it sound like hard work but hard physical work was what her restless body craved right now; she needed to fall into bed each night too tired to think. Too tired to dream. Besides, looking for something in her own line of work would take too much time. She needed to launch straight into a job, no matter if she was over-qualified.

So tomorrow, back in Tavistock, she would get the Truro phone number from Jean, check that work was still available, contact a house agent in Plymouth and put the cottage on their books, and sling her hook. And never, ever look back.

The next few weeks decided, Fen put them out of her mind and tested the temperature of the water with her toes. Chilly enough to take her breath away. No one but the most stout-hearted would take to the Atlantic breakers until midsummer.

But Fen wasn't faint-hearted and she stripped down to her bra and pants and waded in, letting the rollers and breakers buffet her, alternatively fighting them and going with them, glorying in the way her tussle with the elemental force of the ocean drained her tired mind of everything else. And at last, wading back to the shore, her hair slicked to her skull and a million droplets of sea water glittering on her skin, she felt free again. Her own woman again.

And then everything changed and the illusion of freedom blew out of existence because Saul was there, watching her, waiting for her where the waves creamed against the shore. And it all came back again, the wanting, the loving, the desperate need.

And the fear. The fear of the emotional pain he could inflict, the joy he could give and thoughtlessly, carelessly take from her again.

A few scraps of wet silk offered no barriers to hide behind and Fen instinctively crossed her arms over her breasts, wishing the small, virtually inaccessible cove weren't quite so secluded. If people had been in the habit of coming here she wouldn't have gone into the water so scantily clad. If there were other people around she wouldn't have had to face him alone, wouldn't have felt so vulnerable, so much at the mercy of what his eyes alone could do to her...

But she couldn't stand here all day, cold sea water surging around her knees, her arms crossed over her heaving bosom as if she were some improbably Victorian virgin. She walked on, tearing her eyes away from his bleak and unreadable features. But his image was printed on her retina, his tall, strong frame shatteringly sexy in body-hugging white denims and a loose-fitting sleeveless black shirt, standing as solid as one of the granite rocks, his feet slightly apart, thrust into the pockets of his denims, just watching her. Watching her...

Her heart was an excruciatingly insistent hammer, battering her ribcage, and her legs felt as if they were made of cotton wool, but she forced herself onwards, trying to look as if his presence was neither here nor there as far as she was concerned.

He had walked out on her a week ago, trailing bitterness like a black cloud, refusing even to talk to her despite the wild and loving intimacies of the night before. And she wasn't going to forgive him for that, forgive him for treating her like a tramp without a feeling to her name.

Always presuming he wanted to be forgiven, of course. He had probably come back to give her another taste of his bitter contempt. No doubt he would tell her, in his own good time.

Her eyes sliding sideways, she located the discarded clothing she'd left above the high-water mark and wondered if she could reach it, pull the baggy T-shirt over her head before she had to confront him head-on. But no, wouldn't you know it, he had moved since the last time she had looked at him, intercepting her line of retreat, his powerfully intimidating body directly in front of her as she walked on to firm sand.

Slowly, her eyes swept up to meet his. She had never wanted to have to see him again, to increase the anguish, and she didn't want to look into his eyes now, but she couldn't help herself.

His face was as still as if it had been carved from rock; only his eyes gave an indication of his feelings. Just a dark flash of something that might have been pain. Or anger. Whatever, it was gone before she could pin it down and make the right interpretation.

He stared into her eyes for a long, silent moment and her breath sobbed in her lungs. It was, she thought with wild incoherence, as if he were drawing her soul right out of her body and into his own. As if she belonged to him, now and always, and he had come to claim his possession.

Fen shuddered in aching reaction and the tiny, revealing movement brought him to life because he touched her then, taking her hands in his and drawing them down, away from her body, the silver gleam of his eyes only just visible beneath the hooded lids as they claimed unspoken yet undeniable ownership of her virtually naked body.

There was no resistance, none whatsoever. As ever, his presence sapped her will, left her a victim of his power. She closed her eyes, trying not to hear the frantic beat of her heart, concentrating instead on the sound of the sea as it surged against the shore and boomed among the outflung rocks that sheltered the cove, on the closer babble and gurgle of the stream as it sped headlong over its bed of stone and sand to merge with the ocean.

She was like that stream, she thought jaggedly as she felt her body's betrayal, the peaking of her aching breasts as they pushed against the inadequate wet silk covering, the hot, hurting magic of the ache in her womb... Yes, just like that happily gurgling stream she felt herself rushing heedlessly towards an almighty, untamable force, flinging herself into wild and elemental danger, never stopping to consider the aftermath.

But it needn't be like that. She could stop it happening. And she would. She opened her eyes on a snap, meeting the steady, mesmeric regard of his, and said thickly, trying to tug her hands out of his grasp, 'Let me go. I don't know why you came here, and I don't want to know. Please leave.'

But he didn't release her, simply took her hands and wrapped them around his waist, his own arms cradling her close, holding her head gently against his chest.

'Don't fight me, Fen. I made a bad mistake. I hurt you, and I'm sorry.' He felt her shudder of emotion and rained kisses on her face, her neck, and her heart gave an anguished leap.

She couldn't let him hurt her again. He had walked away from her, not giving a damn for her feelings, treating her as if she didn't have any. And maybe he had thought things over, calmed down, and decided to come back for more of what she had so willingly given.

Well, it just wasn't on!

She brought her arms round and pushed at his chest, lashing out verbally, 'Come back for another romp between the sheets, have you? Nothing better to do? Well, I'm sorry, I have!' Far better things to do with her life than endure the kind of pain he could dole out. Maybe his need for her was greater than his reluctance to bed a woman who didn't regard sleeping around as a way of life, a woman who might ask for something more permanent than he was able to give, but, just the same, the time would come when he would again walk away. And the second time, the final time, would be far worse than the first. She would never survive it.

She renewed her ineffectual battering of his chest and he caught her hands between his own, his eyes caressing her flushed and angry face, one brow slowly drifting upwards as she scorned, 'You couldn't move fast enough when you discovered I don't make a career out of being a mistress. Can you only function with a woman you know you can pay off and no hard feelings? Are you frightened of the other type—a woman who would make love with her emotions and not a pocket calculator? She'd be a liability, wouldn't she? She might start asking for things you couldn't give, like love and respect and a normal family life——'

'Don't.' Amazingly, he was smiling. She saw the curve of his mouth just before he cut off her tirade with his kiss. A swift, possessive branding that sent the fight draining straight out of her body, leaving behind a mish-mash of hopes and yearnings, needs and confusions. 'Don't say another word. And put this on.'

Two long strides took him to the little heap of her clothing and in one second more he was tugging the concealing T-shirt over her head.

'That's better.' He brushed her fringe out of her eyes. 'We need to talk and I can't even think straight with all that tempting flesh of yours in front of my eyes. Back to the house, I think.'

Sliding an arm around her waist, he pulled her close and set off slowly towards the head of the cove, and she wondered why she was letting this happen, why her will-power disappeared when he was around, why her need for emotional survival, at all costs, became extinct.

The brush of his thighs against her own as they walked was torture and heaven all rolled into one and when his feet dragged to a halt she was glad to stop, too, and lean against him, her legs too weak to hold her upright.

'I walked away because my pride was shattered,' he said, his voice thick. 'I wasn't thinking straight. Can you forgive me?' He eased her round, pulling her into the heat of his body, his hands looped behind her waist. 'Making love to you had been the most beautiful experience of my life, and all I could think was that you had been laughing at me—letting me believe a lie and thinking what a fool I was. That you must have thought me ridiculous when I started to behave like an amateur psychologist.' He shifted his feet in the sand making her very aware of his physical arousal as his body moved against hers. 'You see, Fen, I thought I understood you, that I knew you—really knew why you were incapable of committing yourself to one man, preferred to play the field, never staying anywhere, or with anyone, for long enough for any real feelings to develop. You must have thought me a pompous fool. And so I walked out. I didn't want to hear you laughing at me.'

Fen couldn't bear to see the bleak residue of pain in his eyes. She traced the severity of his mouth with the tip of one finger, shaking her head.

'I'll laugh with you, never at you. And you weren't wrong. As a psychologist you were doing fine. I didn't sleep around to stop myself becoming emotionally dependent on one man, I never let a man get near me. Or only once, and that was a disaster that simply reinforced my opinion that I was far better off alone. I never wanted to get like my mother. She was so dependent on Dad, so much his creature, that there was nothing of herself left, not even a tiny corner she could give to her child.'

'Yet you made love with me.' He cupped the delicate oval of her face with his hands, his eyes watchful. 'Does that tell me anything?'

Fen shivered. She was treading dangerous ground. Oh, he had told her that the night they had spent together had been the most beautiful experience of his life, that hurt pride had made him walk away from her in bitterness and anger. But that didn't necessarily mean he wanted her in his life for a moment longer than it took for him to tire of her.

'What do you want it to mean?' she prevaricated, gasping as the ball of his thumb slowly rubbed the soft pout of her lips.

'That you've found a man you could live with, that you're not necessarily better off on your own, that giving yourself doesn't mean losing yourself. That you'll marry me.' His eyes searched hers with burning intensity and his voice was rough as he added, 'I'll give you two minutes to think about it. I want you here, and I want you now. But something that beautiful demands a commitment. You've got two minutes. I can't hold out longer than that.'

Two seconds would be more than enough. Tears shimmered in her golden eyes. 'Do you love me?' she asked, unconscious of the wistful plea in her voice.

'Always.' His mouth sealed the statement and Fen responded dizzily, everything inside her going out of control with sheer joy, exploding, and when he demanded, 'And you? Tell me you love me. Tell me you'll marry me,' she could only cling to him, lost in the closeness of him, her voice a tiny patter of sound as she murmured his name, her affirmatives over and over again.

And somehow, without her being truly aware of how they had got there, they were back at the house, the utter silence of drowsy midday surrounding them, and he said as he carried her up the narrow staircase, 'Tomorrow I'll take you home and install you there. We shall be married from there, despite the conventions. We'll leave a note for Alex, pinned on the door, and he can finish up here, do whatever's necessary. But the rest of today, and tonight, my darling, is ours, and ours alone.'

It was almost dark when they emerged at last from the isolated little house, wandering down to the cove, hand in hand, haunted by love, bemused and bewitched by it. Fen felt as if she was walking in a dream, or in paradise, on a journey that would go on until the end of her life, and Saul would walk with her, sharing everything, every splendour and joy.

'You know,' she said lightly as she dropped to the soft sand, gazing out to where the sea should be to view a blanket of black silk, spangled with starshine, a blanket that whispered softly to itself in its sleep, 'I still don't really know how this all happened. Loving each other, I mean.'

'Fate, my darling.' He dropped to his haunches in front of her and she could hear the smile in his voice. 'You must have heard of it. And you can't fight it. When I first saw you I frankly lusted after you and vowed I'd take you from Alex. I wanted you in my life, not his—or any other man's. Then things shifted gear and I started to worry about you, what would happen to you and the rest of your life. I found myself wanting to take care of you, teach you not to be afraid of emotion. Oh, I still wasn't thinking in terms of a lifetime together—I'd been bamboozled by one woman and didn't intend making that mistake again. What I didn't realise was that I was already in love with you, in so deep I couldn't get out, that I would have devoted the rest of my life to you, despite what I believed to be your dubious past.'

He reached out to touch her face, the touch of his hands so tender, she wanted to cry. 'My heart had already accepted that you were an indivisible part of me. And then when you told me you weren't what you seemed I felt—unfairly—that I had been made a fool of yet again. It took a while to get that pride under control and admit that you were the only woman for me, that being made a fool of, as I saw

it, didn't matter a tinker's cuss. That, my darling, is
what fate is. So let's drink to it.'

He had collected a cool-box from the boot of his
car and now he extracted champagne and two tall
crystal glasses. And the liquid exploded in a fountain
of bubbles, just as Fen's love for him exploded within
her heart. He touched his glass to hers and settled
beside her, his mouth a whisper away from hers as he
murmured, 'To fate. And our life together. Our love.'

'Our love,' she echoed, her glass slipping from her
hand, watering the sand with vintage champagne.

Fen didn't notice the loss as she reached up to pull
his dark head down to hers. She didn't need intoxi-
cants, all she needed was Saul, and he left her in no
doubt at all that he was hers for a lifetime as his lips
answered hers with tender promise.

NORA ROBERTS

◆

SWEET REVENGE

Adrianne's glittering lifestyle was the perfect foil for her extraordinary talents — no one knew her as *The Shadow*, the most notorious jewel thief of the decade. She had a secret ambition to carry out the ultimate heist — one that would even an old and bitter score. But she would need all her stealth and cunning to pull it off, with Philip Chamberlain, Interpol's toughest and smartest cop, hot on her trail. His only mistake was to fall under Adrianne's seductive spell.

AVAILABLE NOW   **PRICE £4.99**

W♦RLDWIDE

Next Month's Romances

Each month you can choose from a wide variety of romance with Mills & Boon. Below are the new titles to look out for next month, why not ask either Mills & Boon Reader Service or your Newsagent to reserve you a copy of the titles you want to buy – just tick the titles you would like and either post to Reader Service or take it to any Newsagent and ask them to order your books.

Please save me the following titles:		Please tick	✓
DANGEROUS ALLIANCE	*Helen Bianchin*		
INDECENT DECEPTION	*Lynne Graham*		
SAVAGE COURTSHIP	*Susan Napier*		
RELENTLESS FLAME	*Patricia Wilson*		
NOTHING CHANGES LOVE	*Jacqueline Baird*		
READY FOR ROMANCE	*Debbie Macomber*		
DETERMINED LADY	*Margaret Mayo*		
TEQUILA SUNRISE	*Anne Weale*		
A THORN IN PARADISE	*Cathy Williams*		
UNCHAINED DESTINIES	*Sara Wood*		
WORLDS APART	*Kay Thorpe*		
CAPTIVE IN EDEN	*Karen van der Zee*		
OLD DESIRES	*Liz Fielding*		
HEART OF THE JAGUAR	*Rebecca King*		
YESTERDAY'S VOWS	*Vanessa Grant*		
THE ALEXAKIS BRIDE	*Anne McAllister*		

If you would like to order these books in addition to your regular subscription from Mills & Boon Reader Service please send £1.90 per title to: Mills & Boon Reader Service, Freepost, P.O. Box 236, Croydon, Surrey, CR9 9EL, quote your Subscriber No:................................... (if applicable) and complete the name and address details below. Alternatively, these books are available from many local Newsagents including W H Smith, J Menzies, Martins and other paperback stockists from 11 November 1994.

Name:..

Address:..

....Post Code:..........................

To Retailer: If you would like to stock M&B books please contact your regular book/magazine wholesaler for details.

You may be mailed with offers from other reputable companies as a result of this application. If you would rather not take advantage of these opportunities please tick box. ☐